MI'KMAQ
OF THE
EAST COAST

Robert M. Leavitt

Fitzhenry & Whiteside Limited

MI'KMAQ OF THE EAST COAST

Mi'kmaq Beginnings page 3

The Mi'kmaq of Today page 4

The Mi'kmaq page 9

What Was It Like Before the Europeans Came? page 13

Europeans Arrive in Mi'kma'kik page 37

Beginning of New Ways page 44

Mi'kmaq Land page 55

The 1940s page 59

Mi'kmaq Today page 62

Glossary page 70

Booklist - Credits page 71

MI'KMAQ OF THE EAST COAST
Fitzhenry & Whiteside acknowledge with thanks the support of the Government of Canada
through its Book Publishing Industry Development Program

Canadian Cataloguing in Publication Data
Leavitt, Robert, 1944-
Mi'kmaq of the East Coast
(First Nations Series)
Rev.ed
Previous ed. published under title: Micmac of the east coast.
Includes bibliography references.
ISBN 1-55041-469-0
1. Mi'kmaq Indians - History - Juvenile literature. I. Title. II. Title: Micmac of the east coast. III. Series

E99.M6L42 2000   971.5'004973   C98-931741-2

The publishers wish to acknowledge the assistance of Glenda Redden, former Social Studies Consultant, Nova Scotia Department of Education, and the earlier work *Wejkwapniaq* by Peter Christmas, Executive Director, Mi'kmaq Association of Cultural Studies

Design: Kerry Designs

© 2000 Fitzhenry & Whiteside Limited
195 Allstate Parkway, Markham, Ontario L3R 4T8
No part of this publication may be reproduced in any form, by any means, without permission in writing from the publisher.
Printed and bound in Canada.

10,000 BC	9000 BC	8000 BC	7000 BC	6000 BC	5000 BC	4000 BC	3000 BC	2000 BC	1000 BC	0	1000 AD	2000 AD

MI'KMAQ BEGINNINGS

Mi'kmaq children at the Red Bank reserve on the Miramichi River live in the same area where their ancestors have lived for a very long time. Many children in eastern Canada can go to village cemeteries where their ancestors of two or three hundred years ago lie buried. But at Red Bank there is a *burial mound* more than 2000 years old. A little way up the river are places hundreds of years older, where Mi'kmaq built cooking fires — the bones are still there from ancient meals — and set up their dwellings. Boys and girls today paddle canoes through the same waters and walk over the same land, but otherwise the things they do are quite different from what the Mi'kmaq people of long ago did as children.

Archaeologists are trying to learn all they can about the ancestors of today's Mi'kmaq. They have found many sites in the Maritimes, some of them much older than the ones at Red Bank. They are still trying to find out how the different peoples in the Maritimes long ago were related to one another.

A Note on Mi'kmaq words used in the Book

The word Mi'kmaq, now widely used for the name of the people and their language, is actually the plural of Mi'kmaw (one person). In this book, for ease in reading, "Mi'kmaq" is used in all cases.

Four other Mi'kmaq words are used frequently in the text. Each of these has a different plural ending in Mi'kmaq. For ease in reading, an English-style plural has been adopted, using an s at the end of each Mi'kmaq word.

John Kim Bell is addressing Mi'kmaq students in a class called Aboriginal Entrepreneurship, offered at UNB.

	Mi'kmaq Plural	English-style Plural
wikuom	*wikuoml*	*wikuoms*
saqamaw	*saqama'q*	*saqamaws*
puoin	*puoink*	*puoins*
kinap	*kinapi'k*	*kinaps*

In the same way, 's is used to show possession (e.g., saqamaw's son). In Mi'kmaq, no ending would be used.

THE MI'KMAQ OF TODAY

The Mi'kmaq of today live in the provinces around the Gulf of St. Lawrence. There are Mi'kmaq *reserves* and communities in eastern New Brunswick and in the Gaspe Peninsula of Quebec, in Newfoundland, and throughout Prince Edward Island and Nova Scotia. The Mi'kmaq call their land Mi'kma'kik (meeg-MAH-gee), the Land of the Mi'kmaq.

As far as we know, the Mi'kmaq and their direct ancestors have lived in what is now Mi'kma'kik (including Newfoundland) for at least the past 3,000 years. Before that, many other people lived there who may or may not have been related to the Mi'kmaq.

THE *PALEO-INDIANS*

The earliest people known to have lived in the Maritimes region hunted caribou at a place near present-day Derbert, Nova Scotia more than 10,000 years ago. When these early people, whom we call *Paleo-Indians*, lived in the Maritimes, the land were no forests. Trees grew thickly along rivers and streams, but otherwise the land was mainly treeless *tundra. Glaciers* lay in some of the higher places, and the climate was colder that it is today, with long winters. Strangest of all, many places that are now under water were dry land. You might not recognize a map of the region as it was 10,000 years ago.

Mi'kma'kik includes Nova Scotia, Prince Edward Island, and parts of New Brunswick, Quebec, and Newfoundland.

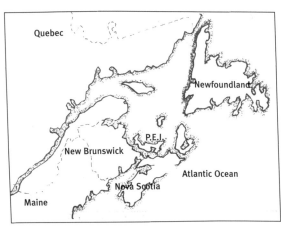

During the last Ice Age, the glaciers covering the Maritimes were so heavy that they pressed down the land. As the glaciers melted and disappeared, beginning about 17,000 years ago, the land began to rise above the level of the ocean, in the way a cushion springs up when you take your weight off it. Of course, the Maritimes rose very slowly — only a few centimetres in a century — but after several thousand years, the land was high enough out of the water that places like Cobequid Bay (near Derbet) and Northumberland Strait were dry land. Prince Edward Island was not an island at all.

After a while, as the glaciers melted away farther and farther to the north, the land there began to rise, too. As this happened, the land to the south stopped rising and began to sink, just as one end of a seesaw goes down when weight is taken off the other end. Today, the Maritime Provinces are still sinking, at an average rate of about 15 cm every century. Areas around the Bay of Fundy and Gulf of St. Lawrence are sinking more quickly than the Atlantic coast of Nova Scotia.

Paleo-Indians who lived inland at Derbert hunted caribou that passed near their camp when *migrating* between flat areas and mountain slopes. Besides eating caribou meat, the Paleo-Indians would have used the skins for clothing and shelter. Many of the stone tools found at Derbert seem to have been made for scraping fat and hair from hides. Other tools were used to cut these hides into desired shapes and to punch holes along their edges so that they could be sewn together.

During the next 7,000 years many changes took place in the Maritimes. Some archaeologists think that from time to time new people moved into the region. Others think that the *ideas* of people from outside the Maritimes, new ways of making tools, weapons, and pottery, may have spread into the area. Both influences may have been felt at different times. We do know that as the centuries passed, people made more and more use of food from the ocean by using better tools, such as *harpoons* and boats, to catch large fish and sea mammals.

Archaeologists have discovered several places near Red Bank, N.B., occupied in ancient times.

A NEW PEOPLE

Archaeologists have found many sites or traces of settlement that are between 3,000 and 4,000 years old. These seem to show that about 3,600 years ago a new people moved up the coast from the area of New England into the Maritimes. They — or their ideas — spread east at least as far as

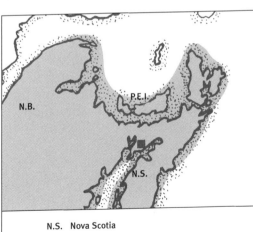

N.S.   Nova Scotia
N.B.   New Brunswick
P.E.I. Prince Edward Island
■   Debert
▒   Extent of land 8000 B.C.

the St. John and Miramichi rivers. People living there, and along the coasts of what is now New Brunswick, fished in the salt water. They made a different type of tool and a new kind of circular house — very much like the house of the Mi'kmaq.

In Nova Scotia, no sites from that time have yet been found which contain the kinds of tools and the houses found in New Brunswick. Yet some archaeologists believe that these ways of making things did spread throughout the region. Because the coastline has been sinking rapidly, places in Nova Scotia where people lived at that time are now under water.

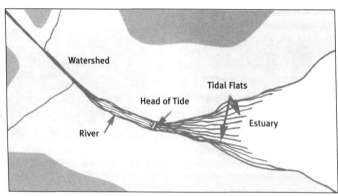

The people who lived along the coasts of the Maritimes would have done most of their fishing and made their camps at river mouths and along estuaries, mainly at the head of the tide, where fish are plentiful. In New Brunswick, on the eastern shore, there are many rivers with long estuaries reaching far inland — like the Miramichi estuary — where sites have been found that date back over 3,000 years. In Nova Scotia, however, where the head of the tide on most rivers is quite close to the ocean, and where long estuaries are rare, people of that time probably lived closer to the sea coast — in places that have washed away or are now under water. But new sites are being discovered in all the Maritime provinces. Each site contains new evidence about the people who have lived in the area during the past 10,000 years or more.

Archaeologists agree that in the past many different people visited the Maritimes. Even if the entire populations did not move, small groups of traders, war parties, and other travellers did move around.

The whole Maritime area has

View from the air of some Mi'kmaq country coastline in Cape Breton today.

| 10 000 BC | 9000 BC | 8000 BC | 7000 BC | 6000 BC | 5000 BC | 4000 BC | 3000 BC | 2000 BC | 1000 BC | 0 | 1000 AD | 2000 AD |

always been a very busy one, with men and women, ideas, goods travelling to and from places on the St. Lawrence River, the Labrador coast, Newfoundland, the Great Lakes, the Ohio River Valley, and southern New England. Archaeologists find out about these ancient travels by looking at the stone tools that people left at their campsites, and at bones and shells of animals that were eaten. From these, they can tell how long ago people lived at a certain site. They notice whether people at other sites were making things in the same way at the same time. For instance, it seems that about 3,700 years ago people over a very wide area from Labrador and Newfoundland to the Bay of Fundy were making the same kinds of tools.

Archaeologists still wonder who the ancestors of the Mi'kmaq were. They may have been the people who came into the Maritimes from the south about 3,600 years ago. Certainly, the Mi'kmaq language is most like those spoken by other Native people in New Brunswick and New England. The Native languages spoken to the north and west are more distantly related.

It is also possible that the ancestors of the Mi'kmaq were people already living in the Maritimes who adopted ideas from people outside the region. Some of those outsiders may also have moved into the region.

MI'KMAQ LANGUAGE

Although they were among the first Native people in North America to meet the Europeans, the Mi'kmaq continue to speak their own language. In many communities children do not speak English or French until they start school.

Mi'kmaq is one of the very large group of *Algonquian* languages

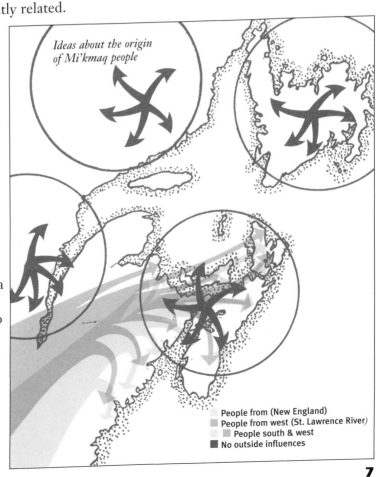

Ideas about the origin of Mi'kmaq people

People from (New England)
People from west (St. Lawrence River)
People south & west
No outside influences

spoken along the Atlantic coast and across the plains to the foothills of the Rocky Mountains. The Mi'kmaq are said to be an Algonquian people. Maliseet-Passamaquoddy, which is spoken in New Brunswick and Maine, is the language most nearly related to Mi'kmaq. Other closely related languages are Penobscot and Abenaki. Some other Algonquian languages spoken in Canada are Cree, Ojibwa, Blackfoot, and Montagnais. The *Iroquoian* languages, such as Mohawk, Cayuga, Onondaga, and Oneida, are not related to Algonquian languages.

> *ARE YOU CURIOUS?*
> Stone tools and pottery were made in the Ohio River Valley, New England, and eastern Canada at different times in the past. Find out what some of them looked like.

DID YOU KNOW?

Although the climate in the Maritimes today is warmer than it was 10,000 years ago, it is not as warm as it was about 5,000 years ago, or even 3,600 years ago. During that period the forests in the Maritimes were mainly hardwood trees, unlike the evergreen forests of today.

1. How has the shape of the Maritime provinces changed in the past 10,000 years?
2. Think about the effects of all the changes in climate. What kind of plants and animals are found today on the tundra?... in the hardwood forests?... in evergreen forests?

In a water-tight basin, make a model of an island. Make part of the shoreline flat — like marshland — and part of it steep. You can use plaster-of-paris, Plasticine, or another water-proof material to build up the island. To show the effect of the island sinking, fill the basin very slowly with water. As the water rises (the same as the land sinking) which parts of the island are covered up the most quickly? Draw a new map of the island each time you make the water 1 cm deeper.

A map of Mi'kma'kik with some Mi'kmaq place names.

What are some ways in which the life of the different Paleo-Indians at Derbert might have been different from the lives of the people in the same area 7,000 years later?

| 10 000 BC | 9000 BC | 8000 BC | 7000 BC | 6000 BC | 5000 BC | 4000 BC | 3000 BC | 2000 BC | 1000 BC | 0 | 1000 AD | 2000 AD |

THE MI'KMAQ

Many people who study about Native peoples think that the early Mi'kmaq must have been like other peoples of Eastern Canada, who depended on hunting in the forests, and a small amount of farming. But the Mi'kmaq did not live this way. If you look carefully at the map of Mi'kma'kik, you will see that the land where they lived had *over 10,000 km of coastline* on the Atlantic Ocean, the Bay of Fundy, and the Gulf of St. Lawrence.

The long coastline, open and rocky in some places, sheltered and sandy in others, supported a great variety of sea life in large amounts. There were so many fish swimming upriver to spawn in the springtime that you might have thought, as an early visitor from Europe did, that you could "walk across the water on their backs". Forests and freshwater lakes were full of game of all kinds and flocks of grouse and passenger pigeons.

Some fur-bearing animals.

1. What is an *estuary?* What life can be found in and around estuaries today?
2. What is a *watershed?* On the map of one of the Maritime Provinces mark the dividing lines between watersheds.
3. What is the *head of tide* on the river? What keeps the tide from going further upstream? Why would the head of tide be a good place to live?

On a map of the Maritime coastline show all the places where rivers and streams empty into the ocean. If you can, mark the head of tide on each one.

The curving coastline and offshore islands of Mi'kma'kik formed many bays. Fish were easily speared or netted there in the sheltered waters, and huge flocks of birds nested on the island rocks. *Tidal flats* were filled with clams, mussels, urchins and flatfish.

As the Mi'kmaq continued to

live in this land, they became separated into groups of people related to one another. Those groups lived along the coast of a bay or in the watershed of a large river. Such a community may have gathered each spring at the head of tide in an estuary, where salt and fresh water meet. The Mi'kmaq knew all the waterways and coastlines of Mi'kma'kik.

VISIBLE AND INVISIBLE WORDS

Mi'kma'kik was only a part of the world the Mi'kmaq knew. It was the visible world, the people, animals, and plants that could be seen. Passing beyond sight to east and south lay the great ocean, and far to the northwest, according to some accounts, beyond the lands of other peoples, was the place where people went after death. A seven year's journey would take you there. Above the stars was a world peopled with beings much like those on Earth but with far greater powers.

The Mi'kmaq felt these powers in the mysterious places of Mi'kma'kik — in caves and on high bluffs. They felt it in thunder and lightning, in earthquakes, rainbows, eclipses, and in changes from the usual cycles of nature — when the salmon did not return in large numbers or when the winter was very mild.

Many beings had *keskmsit* (gess-K'M-zeed), extraordinary personal power. They could bring health or sickness, plenty or famine, success or failure to living beings. Beings with *keskmsit* lived not just among the dead and above the stars; they were also the people and animals and plants of Mi'kma'kik. Living beings — as well as certain trees and plants, natural and made objects — had a spirit, or soul. The spirits of people's belongings went with them after death.

Sometimes a Mi'kmaq man or woman — known as *puoin* (boo-OH-een) or a *kinap* (GEE-nahb) — could use the power of a personal, animal spirit-helper to talk with the spirits of the visible and invisible worlds and learn how they felt and what they were going to do. All the people felt close to the spirits of the animals and plants on which they depended for food, medicine, tools shelter, and clothing.

It was only because the Mi'kmaq treated them with great respect that the animals allowed themselves to be hunted. Their spirits could return to the land of the living in new bodies. The Mi'kmaq did not burn the bones of beaver, moose, caribou, or bear — or allow dogs to eat them. If they did, the animals would be offended and could not be hunted again.

But if the animals were offended, or if people became sick or fought with one another, there were ways to make peace. Men and women who understood the balances between people and animals, between the visible and invisible worlds, and between the powers of different beings could help. *For all Mi'kmaq, the visible and invisible worlds were one.*

> ## ARE YOU CURIOUS?
> Read some stories of the Mi'kmaq to learn more about extraordinary powers and the close ties between people and animals. (See the booklist on pages 71-72).

FUNERAL

Imagine a young Mi'kmaq woman of long ago, who is preparing for her father's funeral. She tells what she and her relatives and friends do to make sure that he will live happily after death.

On the day my father died, we wrapped him up in a soft moosehide decorated with beautiful quillwork and with shell and copper beads. We set his body in a kneeling position facing east, and we continued weeping for many days. We gathered all of my father's possessions, his weapons and tools, his robes and tobacco for burial. Their spirits will go with him.

When that time of mourning was over, we wrapped his body tightly in skins and birchbark and placed him with honour high in

It is four months now since my father died in the coldest part of last winter. Today we are going to bury him on the island where all the graves are.

11

the branches of a tree. Now that the frost is out of the ground he will be buried.

Everyone is coming here for the funeral feast. Men will make speeches about my father. They'll tell about his skill as a hunter, his great strength, and his fine way of making canoes. Someone will recite a list of all his ancestors, and the famous puoins and leaders he is related to. We will be happy that he is with them all.

Each person who comes will bring something valuable to put in my father's grave. He will have these things with him in the land of the souls. People will also bring gifts for my mother and for my uncles, because they no longer have my father's help.

My mother and I are going to live with her brother and his family this summer. They've just had their first child. I can't wait to see him.

1. How might we know about these funeral customs?
2. What things do people do at funerals today? What do they show about our beliefs?

WHAT WAS IT LIKE BEFORE THE EUROPEANS CAME?

We know about the ancient Mi'kmaq by studying the stone tools, animal bones, and other objects found in places where they have lived over the past 3000 years. We also know about their way of life by reading stories of Mi'kmaq people themselves — as told to the first French priests and traders who came to Mi'kma'kik. The French visitors drew pictures of what they saw and wrote about what the Mi'kmaq told them. These accounts all seem to agree with one another.

Before they called these people Mi'kmaq, which wasn't until about 1650, Europeans called them by other names. Two of these were *Souriquois*, used by the French, and *Tarrentines*, used by the English.

The first writer to mention people whom we assume to be Mi'kmaq was Jacques Cartier, who came in 1534; but the most detailed accounts date from the 1600s. Marc Lescarbot, a lawyer from France, travelled in Mi'kma'kik from 1606 to 1607. Father Pierre Biard, a Jesuit priest, stayed from 1611 to 1613 and wrote reports about his work. Nicolas Denys traded furs throughout Mi'kma'kik for over thirty years until he retired in 1668 to the Baie des Chaleurs, where he wrote about his experiences, Father Chrestien LeClercq, a missionary, lived in the Gaspe during the late 1600s and left some accounts of Mi'kmaq life.

These men wrote about the

Mi'kmaq more than 100 years after first contact with Europeans. Much of what they saw and heard showed that European ways had already changed Mi'kmaq life.

It is the right of the head of the nation, according to the customs of the country...to distribute the places of hunting to each individual. * It is not permitted to any Indian to overstep the bounds and limits of the region...assigned him in the meetings of the elders. These are held in autumn and spring expressly to make this assignment. (LeClercq).

*This way of doing things was really started because so many hunters were trying to trap beaver and moose to get furs for trading. Before the Europeans came, chiefs did not decide who hunted where.

Sometimes the French writers showed their own biased attitudes about Mi'kmaq ways:

I have seen them give to the dead man guns, axes iron arrowheads and kettles, for they held all these to be much more convenient...than would have been their kettles of wood, their axes of stone, and their knives of bone, for their use in the other world...It has been troublesome to disabuse them of that practice.**(Denys)

**The Mi'kmaq believed that the souls of the dead would need these things in the land of the dead.

Most of our knowledge about how the ancient Mi'kmaq lived before any Europeans came to Mi'kma'kik is based on what we can learn from these early writings. We also rely on our knowledge of the coastal environment, archaeological findings, and the oral traditions of later Mi'kmaq. Using all of this information together helps us to correct the biases shown by the early writers.

1. Mi'kmaq of the 1600s told French writers about ancient times. How do you suppose they knew what life had been like in the 1400s before the Europeans came?
2. Have you ever found it hard to understand why a person from another culture acts the way he or she does? Give an example.
3. Do you think our knowledge about the ancient Mi'kmaq will continue to improve? Why?

HUNTING AND FISHING ALL YEAR ROUND

What do we know about the Mi'kmaq and their life in Mi'kma'kik before the Europeans came? Did they move about from place to place? Because the Mi'kmaq depended on the ocean for most of their food, they spent most of their time on or near the water. Food can be found there in all seasons of the year.

DID YOU KNOW?

There were no deer in Nova Scotia until the late 1800s. See if you can find out why.

10 000 BC	9000 BC	8000 BC	7000 BC	6000 BC	5000 BC	4000 BC	3000 BC	2000 BC	1000 BC	0	1000 AD	2000 AD

1. What is a run of fish?
2. Where in the water would each type of fish be found?
3. Would all of the animals in the chart have been found throughout Mi'kma'kik? Read about the different animals to find out.
4. What connections can you make between the fish cycle and where the Mi'kmaq lived during each season?
5. Compare the fish cycle with modern legal fishing and hunting seasons for each species. Do you go fishing? What do you do with the catch? Is it necessary to camp or can you go for the day?

ARE YOU CURIOUS?

Find out more about a French explorer, priest or businessman who visited Mi'kmakik in the 1500s or 1600s. How was life in the New World different from his life in France?

Spring Runs	Summer Fishing		Fall Runs	Winter Runs
smelt	mackerel	clam	eel	
herring	cod	quahaug		smelt
sturgeon	shad	oyster	salmon	tomcod
striped bass	capelin	mussel	brook trout	
gaspereau	skate	scallop	herring	*On Winter Ice*
flounder	flounder	sea-		
salmon		urchin		walrus
brook trout	halibut	lobster	(some summer	seal
	plaice	crab	fish offshore)	
	squid	porpoise		

Offshore Islands	In Forested Areas and Open Land near the Coast	In Deep Snow and on Frozen Ponds
		moose
waterfowl	turtles and eggs	caribou
eggs	moose beaver grouse	beaver
	caribou bear nuts & berries	
	hares and other small animals	
	passenger pigeons and geese	

DID YOU KNOW?

From the kinds of bones and shells found at a site, archaeologists can sometimes tell what time of year it was when people lived there. Certain kinds of fish such as tomcod, for instance —would have been caught only during winter runs. Because clams grow faster during the summer than during the winter, the last growth ring on the shell shows the time of year the clam was killed.

The people in a Mi'kmaq community all lived together in the same place for only a short time each spring and fall and for brief summer get-togethers. But they worked together all year round. They shared fish and game, stone for tools, wood, bark and other materials. Because some kinds of food could be found only in certain parts of the community's territory, the Mi'kmaq distributed what they caught. One family might gather shellfish while a second caught flounder or shad; another hunter might bring down a moose. Everyone shared food with relatives and neighbours.

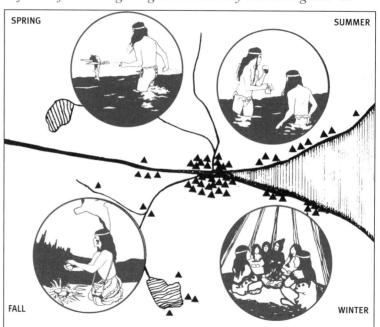

Where the Mi'kmaq lived in the four seasons of the year.

In the *spring* of the year the Mi'kmaq lived together in very large camps near the head of tide on major rivers.

During the *summer* they scattered along the coast in small family groups of one or two dwellings.

Fall found the Mi'kmaq camping along rivers and streams near the coast or farther inland.

In *winter*, some families stayed inland on lake shores. Others returned to the coast, where they lived in small groups as they had during the summer. From the coast, men could make brief hunting trips into the woods — for moose, caribou, or beaver.

WRITING:

1. Begin writing a biography of a Mi'kmaq boy or girl (give your subject a name) living in ancient times.* In Chapter I of your biography you will tell about the place where

your subject lives.

Whatever details you include should be based on what you read in this book and other books.

or

2. Describe the place where a Mi'kmaq girl or boy grew up 500 years ago. List as many ideas as you can.

1. Where did the Mi'kmaq spend most of the year? What brought them together in the spring and fall? Why did they spread out during the summer and winter?
2. Why was it desirable to share food with relatives and neighbours?
3. Have you eaten any of these kinds of fish, birds, or mammals?

Make an imaginary map of the area occupied by a Mi'kmaq community. Think about, and show on the map:
— where the "boundaries" of the community might be
— where different food animals are found
— where people live in each season
— routes of travel between communities

FISHING

Using a few methods, the Mi'kmaq could easily catch great quantities of fish.

At the narrowest place of the rivers, where there is the least water, they make a fence of wood clear across the river to hinder the passage of the fish. In the middle of it they leave an opening in which they place bag-nets...so arranged that the fish run into them. These bag-nets...they raise two or three times a day, and they always find fish therein. It is in spring that the fish ascend, and in autumn they descend and

ARE YOU CURIOUS?

1. Find out about or visit a modern fish weir.
   How is it like the weir described by Nicolas Denys?
2. Find out how a harpoon works. What is the difference between a harpoon and a leister or spear? Why wouldn't you use a spear to catch a very large fish?
3. In the early 1500s, the Mi'kmaq word for *cod* was *pacolos* — a word taken from Portuguese and Basque. How can you explain this word borrowing?
4. It is believed that the Mi'kmaq may have obtained as much as 90% of their food from salt and fresh water. Why would this have been so? Why didn't they do more hunting and gather more wild fruits and vegetables?
5. Which kinds of fish would have been caught in weirs? Which would have been speared or harpooned? How would shellfish have been taken?

Make a model of a *leister* out of wood.

Bag-net to trap fish that come in on the tide.

return to sea. At that time they place the opening of their bag-nets in the other direction. (Denys)

To make the fence for a fish *weir* men drove sticks vertically into the river bottom, about one metre apart. Then, working at the surface of the water, they wove branches across the sticks, pushing them down as they worked until the weir was complete. The bag-nets were woven from twine made from such materials as strips of basswood bark or Indian hemp. Weirs could be set up in salt-water channels as well as in rivers.

Fish spears, or *leisters*, were made by sharpening a piece of bone and attaching it to the end of a long stick. Two side-pieces extended beyond the point to hold the fish once it was stabbed. Fishermen used leisters in shallow water to spear salmon, trout and other kinds of fish that were entering rivers. Harpoons were used to spear seals, small whales, and larger fish, such as sturgeon, which might be three or four metres long.

At the night, fishermen carried their canoes to pools upriver, where they lured salmon with the light of birchbark torches and speared them in the hundreds. Women may have done most of the fishing and shellfish gathering but men and children fished, too.

ARE YOU CURIOUS?

Find out about the life cycles and habits of some of the fish, birds, and mammals listed. What kinds of turtles in Mi'kma'kik are big enough to eat?

Box covered with Mi'kmaq quillwork, made after Europeans came.

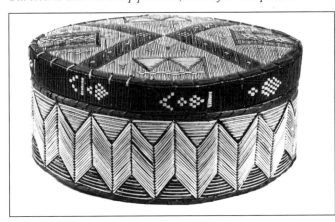

HUNTING

The hunting by the Indians in old times was easy for them. They killed animals only as they had need of them. When they were tired of eating one sort, they killed some of another. If they did not wish longer to eat meat, they caught some fish. They never made an accumulation of skins of Moose, Beaver, Otter, or others, but only as far as they needed them for personal use. (Denys)

The Mi'kmaq hunted in all seasons. They needed animals not only for food, but for materials that they used in many other ways— to make clothing and robes, house coverings, tools, and utensils. *Puoins* made rattles from the dewclaws of moose and medicines from animal glands. Porcupine quills were used to decorate clothing and pouches.

Men hunted moose, caribou, bear, and beaver. Women cleaned the *carcasses* of these animals and birds like geese. Children gathered eggs and caught grouse and other birds by snaring them or clubbing them. Everyone knew that the animals let themselves be hunted to supply people's needs. So they thanked the animals and treated them with respect.

BIRDS

A Mi'kmaq girl tells how she hunts for birds during the spring and summer.

If you know how to walk very quietly and slowly, you can get close enough to a grouse to catch it in a little noose at the end of a stick. You slip the loop over its head and pull it tight. Nothing to it!

Sometimes I go at night in the canoe with my mother. We sneak up among the flocks of seabirds sleeping on the water. We lie down in the canoe and just let ourselves float in among them. They think

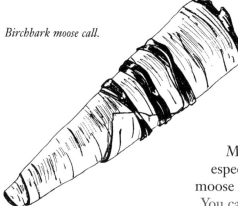

Birchbark moose call.

we're a drifting log. Then we sit up suddenly and light our torches! The birds fly up in confusion. They come so close to the light that we can knock them out of the air with sticks and wring their necks.

MOOSE

Moose was a favourite food of the Mi'kmaq, who hunted them all year long, but especially in the winter. A young man tells about moose hunting.

You can learn how to stalk the moose, telling from its droppings and from the tracks and broken branches how long ago it passed and whether it is male or female, old or young. You track a moose until you are close enough to shoot an arrow. Then you may need to follow the wounded moose and shoot again — and again.

In the fall you can lure the bull by letting water fall into the river from birchbark dish held up high. He will hear the sound and come to the river especially if you call to him with the cow's cry. The call of a bull will lure him too; but he'll be ready to fight!

In the winter, when the crust is on the snow, you can chase a moose with your dogs. The dogs can run on top of the crust, and you have your snowshoes, but the heavy moose sinks through. Even in the summer, dogs can chase a moose and bring it down.

10 000 BC	9000 BC	8000 BC	7000 BC	6000 BC	5000 BC	4000 BC	3000 BC	2000 BC	1000 BC	0	1000 AD	2000 AD

We can use every part of the moose. We eat the meat, the organs, the fat, and marrow. We cook a delicious stew in a wooden kettle by dropping red hot stones into it. We use the bones to make tools and dice. My mother uses moose skins to make clothing, robes, pouches, and coverings for our house.

Moose fat can be melted down, then drunk. When it cools, it thickens and can be stored for some time in a bark box.

BEAVER

The Mi'kmaq hunted beaver by shooting or harpooning them in the water or at their breathing holes in the ice. Another way to get beaver was to destroy their dam, draining the pond and exposing them on the muddy bottom where they were easily shot or speared. Sometimes hunters would make a hole in the ice near a *beaver lodge* to scare beaver into the water. Soon the beaver had to go to their breathing holes, where other hunters waited to kill them. The Mi'kmaq ate beaver meat and used their fur for robes and their sharp teeth for *gouges* and knives.

WRITING:

Chapter II in your biography will describe fishing and hunting trips your subject takes. Include as many details as you can. (Whatever you include should be based on your reading in this and other books.)

Illustrate the chapter with drawings or models.

or

Make drawings of a Mi'kmaq hunting or fishing trip. Include as many details as you can.

1. How did men, women, and children share the work of getting and preparing food? Make a chart to show your answers.
2. How did the Mi'kmaq use the parts of animals they didn't eat? When the Europeans came to Mi'kma'kik, what things would they have had the Mi'kmaq would welcome as improvements on these animal materials?
3. Nicolas Denys seems to find it unusual that the Mi'kmaq didn't kill more animals than

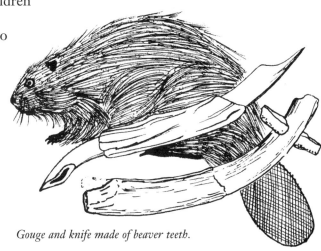

Gouge and knife made of beaver teeth.

they needed, and didn't keep extra skins. Why do you think they didn't? Why do you think Denys found this remarkable?
4. Other European writers were disturbed by the Mi'kmaq giving away or burying possessions at funerals. Why do you think Denys tired to stop the Mi'kmaq from doing this?

WIKUOMS/SHELTER

The Mi'kmaq had portable houses. The frame of a *wikuom* (WEEG-oo-ohm), or house, was left standing when people moved camp. *Wikuom* covers intended for long-term use were carried from place to place. Some *wikuoms* were built for temporary shelter, perhaps even for a single night. The latter were quite small; but seasonal dwellings could be large enough to hold 25 people and might have two or more *hearths*. Although most *wikuoms* had circular floors, larger ones were sometimes oval or rectangular.

The Mi'kmaq usually covered their *wikuoms* with sheets of birchbark, but for temporary shelter they might use hides or firboughs. Sometimes *rush mats* were used to line a *wikuom* or were spread on the floor. In the summer the Mi'kmaq may have used rush mats to cover permanent *wikuoms*. The mats were skilfully woven to shed rain.

MOVING DAY

In the spring a young woman helps move her family's belongings from their camp

to a site a day's walk east along the coast. They will spend the coming summer there, fishing from canoes and gathering eggs and hunting for birds on a nearby island.

It's time to leave. We've had a wonderful time here, seeing all our relatives, feasting and dancing. I like it best when we are all camping together. Everything is coming to life again after the winter. Everyone is glad for the long days. I think the fish must swim upriver just to be in the shallow water, where they can splash and jump together in the sunshine.

Soon we'll all be moving for the summer. A day's walk east of here is the place where we usually set up our wikuom. There's a small beach and a brook that comes from a beaver pond a little way up into the woods. Offshore, there is a rocky island where thousands of birds nest — gulls and terns, seaducks, puffins, auks, and guillemots. What a noise they make! But eggs are delicious, and we can catch all the ducks we need for eating. My father will make me a whistle from the duck's hollow leg-bone.

It's never lonely there. Often, friends paddle by to visit, bringing us clams or fish. We give them eggs or birds our friends stay all day, and sometimes at night we all go birdhunting together. Then we make a stew in the wooden kettle near the beach. I love the sound of the red-hot rocks hissing as they are dropped into the broth.

My father and mother made the kettle there before I was born. It's really a big hole carved into the top of a fallen log. This kind of kettle takes several days to make. You have to make a fire on top of the log, so that part of it burns. Then you chop and cut that away with bone and stone tools then you build a fire again, and chop again — over and over until the hole is deep enough to cook in. Before you make a kettle like that, be sure it's in a good place — because you can't move it! My parents knew that someone would always be coming here to take advantage of the bird island, and that they'd need to cook big meals.

I think that the best part of moving is setting up the *wikuom*, with fresh fir boughs on the floor. Sometimes there are new birch-bark covers to decorate. This year, we'll have two *wikuoms* on the beach: my sister and her husband are going to stay with us all summer. She and I will help Mother set up the camp as soon as we arrive, while the men start making the fish weir. It will be so much fun to play with my little nieces and nephews, making toys for them and carrying the baby around in her cradleboard wherever we go. Children are wonderful. We all love them and do anything we can for them, so they are always happy. I can hardly wait!

Nicolas Denys described how a Mi'kmaq camp was set up.

Kettle burned and carved in a tree trunk.

After they have lived for some time in one place, which they have beaten for game all around their camp, they go and camp fifteen or twenty *leagues* (75-100 km) away. Then the women and girls must carry the *wikuom*, their dishes, their bags, their skins, their robes, and everything they can take, for the men and the boys carry nothing, a practice they follow still at the present time.

Having arrived at the place where they wish to remain, the women must build the camp. Each one does that which is her duty. One goes to find poles in the woods; another goes to break off branches of Fir, which the little girls carry. The woman who is mistress, that is, she

23

who has borne the first boy, takes command, and does not go to the woods for anything. Everything is brought to her. She fits the poles to make the *wikuom* and arranges the Fir to make a place for each person. This is their carpet...

They lined all the inside of the *wikuom* to four fingers' depth, with the exception of the middle, where the fire was made, which was not so lined. They arranged it so well that it could be raised all as one piece. It served them also as mattress and as pillow for sleeping... If the family is a large one they make the wikuom long enough for two fires; otherwise they make it round, just like military tents, with only this difference that in place of canvas they are of barks of Birch. These are so well fitted that it never rains into their *wikuoms*. The round kind holds ten to twelve persons, the long twice as many. The fires are made in the middle of round kind, and at the two ends of the long sort. (Denys, 1672)

1. How did the Mi'kmaq share the work of moving camp and setting up *wikuoms?*
2. Denys mentions that "the men and boys carry nothing" when the Mi'kmaq moved camp. How might you explain this?
3. What would be the diameter of a *wikuom* in which ten or twelve people could sleep?

Build a large model of a Mi'kmaq *wikuom*. Compare the amount of indoor space Mi'kmaq people had long ago with the amount people usually have today. How would your life be different if your home were so small? Think about advantages and disadvantages.

Setting up Camp.

WRITING:

Chapter III of your biography will tell what it is like for your subject to wake up one morning in a new camp. (Whatever you include should be based on what you read in this book and other books.)

1. What might it have been like for a Mi'kmaq boy or girl to wake up one morning in a new camp? Tell about a similar experience that you have had.
2. The early French visitors thought the wooden kettles were inconvenient because the Mi'kmaq had to camp where they had made the kettles. What would the Mi'kmaq have said to that?

BIRCHBARK

The Mi'kmaq valued the bark of the paper birch for its wonderful and practical qualities. It is easily cut and sewn without risk of splitting. It is light in weight, flexible, and does not shrink as it dries. It can be made as then as paper or used in sheets up to one centimetre thick. Birchbark contains a kind of wax, which makes it resistant to water, rotting, and insects. This wax also makes birchbark flammable.

These are some things the Mi'kmaq made from birchbark:

wikuoms	cooking pots	kindling
canoes	dippers	torches
bowls	sap-collectors	tobacco
boxes	canoe-bailers	pipes (!)
raincapes	wrappings	

Birchbark must be harvested carefully. It is strongest and toughest when the sap is flowing in the tree. Then the inner rind sticks to the bark so that bark and rind can be peeled off in a single sheet. During a long thaw in winter or when the sap began to run in the spring, the Mi'kmaq removed the bark from the tree by making a long vertical slice with a sharp stone blade. They peeled it away from the cut by prying it loose with short sticks all the way around the tree. The top

Bowls and containers made of birchbark.

25

and bottom edges of the piece did not have to be cut — they followed the horizontal grain of the bark.

After removing the bark, the Mi'kmaq rolled it up at right angles to its natural curl and inside out, heating it slightly with a torch or hot water to make it more flexible than usual. The bark had to be kept damp if it was not going to be used right away. If it dried out, it would become brittle and split.

BIRCHBARK CANOES

Steps in Making a Canoe (adapted from Denys)

For making their canoes they sought the largest Birch trees they could find. They removed the bark of the length of the canoe, which was of three to four fathoms and a half (6 to 9 m) in length. The breadth (of the canoe) was about two feet (60 cm) in the middle. The depth was such that for a man seated it came up to his armpits. The lining inside for strengthening it was of slats, of the length of the canoe and some four inches (10 cm) broad, lessening towards the ends in order that they might match together. These slats were made of Cedar, which is light, and which they split in as great lengths as they wished, and also as thin as they pleased. They also made from the same wood half-circles to form ribs, and gave them their form in the fire.

For sewing the canoe, they took roots of Fir (black spruce) of the thickness of the little finger, and even smaller; they were very long. They split these roots into three or four parts. They made these into packages, which they placed in the water for fear they might dry up. There were also necessary two sticks of the length of the canoe, entirely round, and of the thickness of a large cane (for making the *gunwales*), and other shorter sticks of Beech (for making the *thwarts*). All these things being ready, they took their bark and bent and fixed it in the form the canoe should have; then they placed the two long pieces all along and sewed them to the rim inside with these roots. (These are the gunwales).

To sew (the gun wales on) they pieced the bark with a punch of pointed bone and passed through the hole an end of the wicker (spruce root), drawing and tightening the stick as closely as they could against the bark, and always wrapping the stick with

Begining to make a canoe.

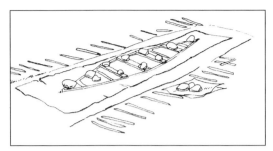
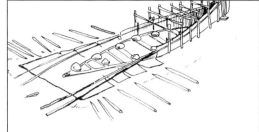

the wicker.

The sticks being well sewed on all along, they placed also the smaller pieces of beech crosswise, one in the middle, entering at its two ends into holes made in the gunwales and three others in front of it. Three others were also placed behind it. All these pieces entered at their ends into holes which were made in the (gunwales), to which they were so firmly attached.

Then are placed in position (lengthwise) those big slats with which they lined all the interior of the canoe from top to bottom, and they were all made to touch one another. To hold them in place, they put over them those (ribs), the ends of which were brought to join on both sides below (the gunwales). They drove these in with force, and they lined all the canoe with them from one end to the other. this made the canoe stiff to such a degree that it did not yield at any point.

There were seams in it, for in order to narrow it at the two ends, they split the bark from above downwards; they then overlapped the two edges one over the other, and sewed them. But to prevent the seams from admitting water, the women and girls chewed the gum of the Fir every day until it became a salve which they applied by aid of fire all along the seams, and this tightened them better than pitch. All this being done, the canoe was finished, and it was so light that a single man could carry it on his head. (Denys)

A birchbark canoe is sealed with fir gum.

DESIGN

Mi'kmaq canoes were shaped differently from those made by other people in North America. The bow and stern had a rounded profile, and the sides of the canoe were highest amidships. Mi'kmaq canoes also tended to be wider at the waterline than at the gunwales. They were remarkably light, and could be paddled swiftly.

27

> *ARE YOU CURIOUS?*
>
> Find out what birchbark is like. How are the layers different from the outside to the inside?
>
> The Mi'kmaq usually placed the inner, brown layer of the bark on the outside of the canoes, *wikuoms*, and containers they made. Why?
>
> Find out where paper birches grow in North America. Who else used birchbark? Did they make similar items? How has birchbark been used by European settlers in North America?
>
> *Make a model canoe. Try to use as many real details as you can. You might like to make a series of models, showing the different stages of making a canoe.*

MEMBERS OF THE COMMUNITY

A *kinap* (GEE-nahb) was a person who had extraordinary strength or skill. When there was a conflict with a neighbouring people, the *kinaps* would advise the community and lead raids. The Mi'kmaq did not engage in actual wars, but they feuded with people who had insulted or injured a relative or friend.

A *puoin* (Boo-OH-een) was a man or woman who had power to communicate with the unseen world. *Puoins* usually carried a medicine bag containing bones, pebbles, carved figures, and other objects that helped them and their extraordinary powers. They could locate game and fish, forecast the weather, and know what other powerful beings were doing. With medicines and ceremonies they could cure illness or remedy harm that those other powers caused. People in the community respected *puoins* and *kinaps* and gave them gifts for their help. Boys or girls who showed signs of having unusual powers might be sent to live with *puoin* or *kinap* to be educated.

A *saqamaw* (SAH-h'm-ow) was a highly respected man in the community, whose advice people valued. Today, the word *saqamaw* means "chief", and the first European visitors often described *saqamaws* as "kings" and thought of them as commanders.

In ancient times, however, Mi'kmaq leaders were members of the community who had gained influence and respect, not power. They could not tell people what to do.

Saqamaws had to be modest, generous, wise, and well spoken. They were often expert hunters and fishermen, who could be expected to know where game animals and fish would be found. People in the community would go to a *saqamaw* for advice about where to set up their *wikuoms*, and they trusted him to suggest a good spot. But the saqamaw did not assign places — he only mentioned them. Because he was so highly respected, he was able to use his influence to organize hunting and fishing for everybody's benefit.

Families might send their sons to live in a *saqamaw's* household and learn from him. The young men would give everything they caught to the *saqamaw*, who would use some of it to feed his very large "family" and give away the rest. In this way, everyone in the community could share all the different kinds of fish, meat, and other foods found in their watershed.

The Europeans thought that the son of a *saqamaw* would automatically become a *saqamaw* himself if he had the ability. Actually, a young man living in a *saqamaw's* household would be likely to have the qualities of a *saqamaw*, but he might not be the *saqamaw's* own son. The *saqamaw* would have called many boys *kwi's* (gweez), that is, "son" — his own sons, his brother's sons, the sons of his male first cousins, and his adopted sons.

A man might be *saqamaw* and *kinap*, and perhaps *puoin* as well. Such a person would have great respect, and might be known throughout *Mi'kma'kik* because many people would seek his help.

Saqamaws, *puoins*, and *kinaps* all were honoured in the community. Other men and women treated them with respect, gave them gifts, and saved the best cuts of meat for them at feasts. In return, these leading men and women served the interests of the whole community.

1. Compare a *kinap* with a modern leader.
2. Was a *saqamaw* a ruler? Did people in the community obey him? Was anyone in *charge* of a Mi'kmaq community?
3. Compare a Mi'kmaq boy's or girl's education with yours. How do you think children who did not go to live with a *puoin*, *saqamaw*, or *kinap* were educated? What did they need to learn?
   What adult in your community would you want to work with or live with for your education if you were not going to school?
4. Why did *saqamaws* have to be modest, generous, and well spoken?
5. Why did the Europeans think of chiefs as commanders?

Kinap, puoin, and saqamaw were important people in any Mi'kmaq community.

FEASTING

A young man recalls the special days in his life and some of the great people he has met.

I love to eat. A kettle full of moose stew or delicious clams, a basket of juicy blueberries, strips of smoked salmon — we know how to make a stomach happy! Now I have travelled to many places and stayed with many remarkable men, but what I remember best are the wonderful feasts we shared at their wikuoms. Often we ate for days at a time, listening to stories, speeches, and songs about all the creatures of Ma'kma'kik sharing a good life together. The first feast I remember is one my uncle gave when his son's first tooth came — welcoming him to the world of chewing! I must have been about four years old. All I remember is the faces of my uncles all around the *wikuom* — chewing on fish and grinning, to the delight of my little cousin. Later that summer there was another feast. This time it was my cousin's first step.

My aunts were cooking caribou stew in the log kettle and roasting fish on sticks by the fire. I also remember a big bear-roast hanging on a twisted cord. It turned round and round and the flames danced about it. All around the fire there were men and women dancing to the beat of the *jikmaqan* (JEE-g'm-ah-'n), a folded piece of bark used as a rattle. I think my little cousin learned to dance before he learned to walk!

The summer I was six years old, I killed my first animal — a small porcupine that I spotted near our *wikuom*.

My father was a good fisherman and hunter, but he was a man who liked to live by himself with his own family. We stayed only a short time at the spring and fall fishing camps, and usually there were just the five of us living in a single *wikuom*. But that day two of my older cousins had stopped by to bring us some flounder. So we had a proper feast after all.

My mother boiled the porcupine meat in a birchbark pot with hot stones. It smelled so good with little drops of seal oil floating on

| 10 000 BC | 9000 BC | 8000 BC | 7000 BC | 6000 BC | 5000 BC | 4000 BC | 3000 BC | 2000 BC | 1000 BC | 0 | 1000 AD | 2000 AD |

the broth that I was almost sorry that I, as the hunter, wouldn't be able to eat any of my first kill. We ate the flounder while they enjoyed the porcupine. I was so happy and proud to be giving this food to my cousins — food that I had caught! They were quite solemn, remember, and said that I would be a great hunter with the bow. My father made up a song about my perfect aim.

When I was fourteen, my father sent me to spend the summer with his brother. This uncle was a well-known *saqamaw*, who had many young men in his household. I wound up staying with him for two-and-a-half years.

At the end of my last summer with him, I killed my first moose. Now that was a feast! For the first time I could eat what I had killed. There were the roasted moose and moose stews, dozens of fish fillets roasting on sticks, and smoked duck and goose boiling in bark pots. I could hardly carry the large tray my aunts piled up with the moose meat. I served it so proudly, first giving my grandfather a slice of the heart and a piece of the tenderest cut. How we ate and laughed! I drank a whole dishful of melted moose fat just to show off.

Things changed for me at the feast. Now that I had killed a moose, I could sit with the men when they talked about our community. I could get married if I liked and have my own wikuom. But I didn't want to get married yet. I wanted to see more of Mi'kma'kik.

My uncle had been planning to take a trip by canoe from our home in Unama'kik (OON-ah-mah-geeg) — Cape Breton — to visit a famous *saqamaw* in Epekwitk (eh-BEH-gweetk) — Prince Edward Island — a trip he had put off because of my first moose feast. Now he invited me and my father to go with him and the others. We would be gone for a month. Meanwhile my mother and sisters would go up the river with my uncle's family to the eel weirs. I dreamed that night about the stacks of smoked eel that would greet us when we got back.

The old *saqamaw* we were going to visit had such great *keskmsit* and amazing strength that no one had ever heard of his equal. In his youth he had travelled to Iroquois and Abenaki territory, where he had fought single-handed against two parties of warriors. He had wrestled with great *puoins* and beaten them. He could take the shape of a bear or a fierce hawk.

At the same time he was a very gentle and soft spoken man. It seemed to me when I first saw him that he would be happy to sit by the fire all day and joke with his grandchildren.

My uncle had come to visit this *saqamaw* to give him moose-hides and porcupine quills, for there are very few moose and no porcupines in Epekwitk. He also wanted to get a certain medicine plant that grew there. He would have

32

10 000 BC	9000 BC	8000 BC	7000 BC	6000 BC	5000 BC	4000 BC	3000 BC	2000 BC	1000 BC	0	1000 AD	2000 AD

a chance to share news from Unama'kik and hear about what was going on to the west.

    The *saqamaw* and his large household — he had several dozen relatives with him — welcomed us with a daylong feast of island fish, smoked, roasted, stewed, and baked. I don't think I have ever seen so many kinds of fish at one meal. There were seven log kettles and as many fires, each tended by a group of women and young girls. On low wooden racks they were also smoking split fish under caribou hides. Later they gave us this smoked fish, packed in birchbark boxes, to take home with us. Its delicious aroma was with us all the way back.

Then we were greeted at home with a banquet of smoked eel! Ah well, we would have plenty of fish all winter.

I returned to my parents' *wikuom* for the winter. During the next few years I spent time staying with my cousins and uncles. Last spring I saw the girl I wanted to marry. My father spoke to her parents and it was arranged for me to go and live with her family for a year. As if they didn't already know that any *wikuom* I lived in would never lack for food!

Today is our wedding. Once again I will have the honour of serving meat that I have hunted. We will set up our own wikuom this summer, and then I think we will feast and feast and feast... for all the years to come.

1. What were the special occasions of a Mi'kmaq man's life?
2. Why do you suppose a young boy's family couldn't eat his first kill? Later, he could eat the first moose he killed.
3. Why did a young man live with his bride's family for a year before they were married.
4. Why was it an honour to serve meat?
5. Even though the Mi'kmaq may have eaten feasts like those the young man describes, they were, as far as we know, slim and well-built people. How can you explain this?

A PUZZLE

    Many of the early writers' accounts mention that winter could be a time of starvation for the Mi'kmaq if hunting was poor. Yet we are also told that the Mi'kmaq knew how to preserve meat, fat, fish, nuts, and berries. What do you think?
1. Maybe the Mi'kmaq didn't starve.
2. Maybe they didn't know how to preserve food, or they couldn't preserve it long enough.
3. Maybe accounts of hunger and starvation refer to the time *after* the Mi'kmaq had begun trading furs with the Europeans in the late 1500s. If this is true, then — either

33

— The Mi'kmaq didn't have time to lay in supply of food for the winter because they were too busy trapping

or

— before the Europeans came, the Mi'kmaq did not depend on hunting in the winter. The fur trade forced them to hunt all winter, taking them away from the coast, where their preserved food was stored. Ordinarily they would have gone hunting inland only in good weather.

Talk about these ideas with your classmates.

KLUSKAP

Kluskap (GLOOS-kahb) is the one who made the earth a good place for Mi'kmaq to live in. He made the mountains and waters, the lakes and islands. Kluskap made each animal the shape and size it is now. He taught people to live wisely, without bragging or trying to have power over others. He showed them which plants could be used as medicines. Although Kluskap is not known from the early records of European visitors to Mi'kma'kik — in fact, he is not mentioned in writing before the 1800s — he is an important figure in Mi'kmaq (and Maliseet) beliefs.

A TRADITIONAL MI'KMAQ STORY

UNCLE MIKJIKJ, THE TURTLE

Kluskap goes by canoe to visit his uncle Mikjikj (MEEK-cheekch) at Piktuk (BEEK-toog). Although Mikjikj is very slow and lazy, he is so good-natured that Kluskap loves him. He decides to make him into a tough and important man. There is to be a feast in the village. "I'm going to stay here," says Kluskap to his uncle, "but you join in. All the girls will be there, and you ought to find yourself a wife. You shouldn't live by yourself."

"That's fine for you to say," Mikjikj complains. "You're so handsome and well dressed. Look at me! I'm so poor that I don't even have one thing good enough to wear to a feast."

"Oh," says Kluskap, "is that what you're worried about? One who has *keskmsit* finds it easy to change clothing. It's harder to change the insides of a person. But before I leave Piktuk, I will do both. Here — put on my belt!"

Mikjikj wraps the belt around his waist. Suddenly, he is wearing the finest clothing. He is a strong and handsome young man. Off he goes to the feast.

Now the *saqamaw* at Piktuk has three beautiful daughters. Mikjikj sees the youngest one at the feast, and he wants to marry her. But all the other young men are jealous of him because they've been wanting to marry this girl, too. They'll kill Mikjikj if he wins her.

Kluskap goes to the *saqamaw's wikuom* to make a proposal of marriage on behalf of Mikjikj. Mikjikj is accepted, and he marries the *saqamaw's* daughter. They live together happily although Mikjikj is still lazy.

One day there is a ball game with a great crowd of young men. "They'll try to trample you," Kluskap warns his uncle, "but I will help you escape. You will be able to jump over your father-in-law's *wikuom* three times. I'm afraid that the third time will go badly for you, but what must be must be."

The young men do try to kill Mikjikj, but he flies over their heads. On the third jump, however, his shirt catches on the *wikuom* poles. He hangs in the smoke, which begins to harden his skin and scorch it. He is very angry. "Kluskap, you're killing me!"

"Not so, my uncle," says Kluskap. "I am making you a great *saqamaw* — the *saqamaw* of turtles. You will have a long life. From now on you'll be able to roll in the fire. You can live on land and in the water. Why, even if your head is cut off, you'll still live for nine days."

Well, Mikjikj is happy. He thinks these talents will be very useful.

Kluskap smokes him until his skin is hard. The scorching can still be seen today. Mikjikj becomes a turtle.

"Of course," Kluskap says, "the young men here still want to kill you. They'll try to burn you — let them! Then they'll try to drown you. Fight them as hard as you can! Say, 'Don't do that!' They'll want to do it even more."

Mikjikj bids Kluskap farewell. As he walks through the village, the young men grab him and throw him into a fire. Mikjikj rolls over — and falls asleep! He is lazy, you know. When the fire burns out, he wakes up. "More wood," he calls. "I'm cold."

So the young men seize him and drag him down to the water. "No!" he screams, "No! Don't do that!" He tears up trees, roots, and huge boulders all the way to the shore. But they load him into a canoe, and far out to sea they throw him into the water. He sinks like a stone.

In the morning, two young men catch sight of something moving on a little island offshore. They paddle out to see what it is. There lies Mikjikj, calmly sunning himself. He slides into the water as they approach, and that is the last they see of him.

Many years later, Kluskap goes to visit Mikjikj and his wife. They have a child, and he is crying.

"I can't understand what he's talking about," says Mikjikj. "Maybe he's speaking sky language." "No," Kluskap answers. "He's talking about eggs. Listen — Wa! Wa!" That's what the Mi'kmaq call an egg today — *waw* (wow). Kluskap decides to play a joke on Mikjikj. "Dig in the sand," he tells him. "There you will find all the eggs you want."

Mikjikj is pleased. And today turtles still lay their eggs in the sand.

1. What does the story of Mikjikj tell you about some Mi'kmaq customs? Why might a Mi'kmaq woman have told this story to her grandchildren?
2. Do you think Mikjikj learns anything?

Illustrate the story of Kluskap and Mikjikj.

EUROPEANS ARRIVE IN MI'KMA'KIK

The Mi'kmaq may have seen men from Europe as early as the beginning of the 1500s, when Basque, Portuguese, English, and Breton fishing boats were coming to shore for water and repairs. Over the next 150 years, as the fishing fleet grew, ships made regular visits to the coast, particularly to Newfoundland. They landed frequently on Cape Breton Island. The Mi'kmaq were friendly to these early visitors, and they were eager to give them gifts of furs in exchange for iron, cloth, copper kettles, and other items. They found these things easier to use than their own stone tools, hide clothing, and dugout cooking pots. The exchange of gifts soon developed into active trading.

It is hard to imagine what the Mi'kmaq of the early 1500s might have thought about the strange boats and bearded men who came to Mi'kma'kik. The newcomers had great *keskmsit:* their large ships, guns, mirrors, and iron tools must have seemed magical. On the other hand, the Mi'kmaq were puzzled by the visitors' desire for furs, which were of no special value to the Mi'kmaq. And they were amazed that, of all the kinds of fish available, fishermen wanted only cod.

Map of Canada, New France, Terra Nova, and Acadia, which included much of what was Mi'kma'kik.

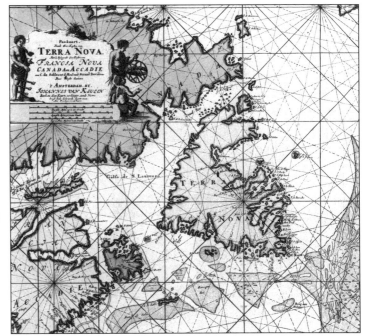

37

Around 1550, fishermen changed their way of preparing cod to take it back to Europe. They had been packing the fresh fish in salt; now they learned to split the cod and dry it in the sun. Their fishing boats could hold more of the lighter dried fish. With this new method, the fishermen did not have to bring a supply of salt with them, so they had more room for trade items. They had more time for trading, too, when they came ashore to dry the cod, a job which took at least a month in good weather.

Hats made of beaver felt had become popular in Europe and large numbers of beaver *pelts* were needed. Skins that the Mi'kmaq had used as clothes for a year were especially useful because all the guard hairs had been worn off. This made the skins easier to turn into felt. The fur trade — still only a sideline of the fishing trade — grew rapidly. By the middle of the 1700s there were hardly any moose or furbearing animals left on Cape Breton Island, Prince Edward Island, or in the Gaspé Peninsula.

The main trading centres where Europeans worked and lived were in Newfoundland and the Gulf of St. Lawrence. Even in 1600, fishing and trading in Nova Scotia had not spread much west of Cape Breton Island, and Native peoples on the Maine coast continued to make use of stone tools. Although there were fishing stations, there were still no permanent European settlements anywhere in Mi'kma'kik.

European method of curing and drying cod.

10 000 BC	9000 BC	8000 BC	7000 BC	6000 BC	5000 BC	4000 BC	3000 BC	2000 BC	1000 BC	0	1000 AD	2000 AD

ARE YOU CURIOUS?
1. Find out more about the beginnings of the fishing industry in North America. Why was cod so valuable to the Europeans?
2. Find out more about the beginnings of the fur trade in North America. What is *beaver felt*?
3. Why were the Mi'kmaq surprised at the Europeans' interest in furs and cod?
4. What were the effects on the Mi'kmaq when the Europeans stopped packing cod in salt and started drying it?
5. What is an epidemic?
6. Think about those Mi'kmaq who caught the diseases without ever having seen a European. How might they have explained the epidemics?
7. Think about how diseases and death would have changed Mi'kmaq life. How would fishing and hunting, travelling, and trading have been affected?

What seemed to have been casual contact with Europeans had already had bad effects on the Mi'kmaq. The very first fishermen and traders who came to Mi'kma'kik carried new diseases with them.

Flu	Measles	Typhoid	Pneumonia
Colds	Chicken Pox	Whooping Cough	Scarlet Fever
Diphtheria	Dysentery Plague	Strep Infections	

The Mi'kmaq, who had never suffered from these diseases, had no *immunity* to them. *Epidemics* spread quickly, often several diseases at once. These would be followed in turn by another group of diseases, leaving the Mi'kmaq no time to develop any resistance. During the first hundred years after European arrival, 75 percent of all Mi'kmaq died. Those who were left found their whole world crumbling around them.

PUOINS AND PRIESTS

A young Mi'kmaq man living in the 1600s tells what he thinks about the European newcomers. The effects of European diseases have reached their peak.

This is a very difficult time. So many of my friends and relatives have died from the new sickness. The *puoins* could not cure them. Even my brother-in-law, a powerful *puoin*, was killed by this disease. To me, it seems that the *puoins* have lost their power.

The people say that the French priests— the ones they call "Father" — have much greater power than our *puoins*. Some Mi'kmaq put their faith in the priests now. Even *puoins* could not cure them. Even my brother-in-law, a powerful *puoin*, was killed by this disease. To me, it seems that the *puoins* have lost their power.

The people say that the French priests — the ones they call "Father" — have

39

much greater power than our *puoins*. Some Mi'kmaq put their faith in the priests now. Even *puoins* imitate them. They have put pictures and strings of beads in their medicine bags — like the things the priests carry.

The other Europeans — the traders and fishermen — are foolish. They brag about their wonderful country across the ocean, yet they have taken a long and dangerous journey to escape from it. They tell us how rich they are, but they complain about even the lowest prices, and they beg for worn-out beaver furs!

The priests are different. I once asked Great-grandfather what it is about priests that sets them apart from the traders and fishermen. He says that a priest is a lot like a *puoin*. They both have spirit helpers they talk with. The priests call this "praying". The priest is the one who cures the sick. Sometimes he touches the sick person with his cross, just the way a *puoin* uses the bones in his medicine bag. Last year, a saqamaw on the mainland prayed with a priest for food. The next day a herd of seals was seen just outside the village.

Great-grandfather says the reason some people believe in the priests now is that the priests are protected by their power from the diseases, which kill even the *puoins*. He thinks that people don't really listen to what the priests are saying in their prayers, but they see the power of the spirit helpers.

A priest and a puoin. Compare their clothes and religious articles.

1. In trading furs, the traders and the Mi'kmaq each thought they were getting a good bargain for themselves. What did each group think the other was getting?
When is something "valuable"?
2. Why didn't the priests seem as foolish to the Mi'kmaq as the other Europeans did?
3. How was the standing of the *puoins* affected by European diseases?

SAQAMAWS AND FISHERMEN

The young Mi'kmaq man of the 1600s tells how his com-

10 000 BC	9000 BC	8000 BC	7000 BC	6000 BC	5000 BC	4000 BC	3000 BC	2000 BC	1000 BC	0	1000 AD	2000 AD

munity has changed since his Great-grandfather's time.

Our *saqamaw* today is very different from the *saqamaw* in Great-grandfather's time. He seems to care more for the European fishermen than for us. They treat him with great honour. They salute him with guns when he visits them, and they give him presents. This makes him seem very important to all the people in our community, and in fact he is very important because he is the only one the Europeans will trade with. We have to give the *saqamaw* our furs, then he passes them on to the traders, giving us the European goods in exchange. He gets to keep a share of these goods for himself, although he is careful not to show them off.

> **ARE YOU CURIOUS?**
> Find out why some French priests came to Mi'kma'kik and other parts of the New World.

Great-grandfather tells me that in his day *saqamaws* and the people all decided together where each family would hunt and fish. Sometimes the *saqamaws* suggested a place for a family, but without any pressure.

In Great-grandfather's day hunters sometimes brought their catches to a *saqamaw*, and he shared the meat among the people. He was a man everyone respected, and they took it for granted that he would be fair and unselfish. Now it seems that the Europeans decide who will collect furs and give out the goods. People can't expect a fair share — it depends on what they bring to the *saqamaw*. I hear that in some places the Europeans are trading through men who are not even *saqamaws*.

Yesterday and this morning, our *saqamaw* and a group of the older hunters decided where families will hunt this winter. Each family is going to have a small hunting area to itself, and no one else will be allowed to hunt there. Of course, everyone is forced to kill as many animals as possible in order to have enough furs to trade for all the things the family needs — beans, flour, ammunition, knives...I won't be surprised if all the beaver in this part of the country are killed off within the next few years.

1. Explain how the job of the *saqamaw* in the community changed during the days of the fur trade. What were new duties? To whom was the *saqamaws* responsible — Europeans, Mi'kmaq, or both?
2. Why might the Europeans have traded through men who were not *saqamaws*?
3. Why did the Mi'kmaq need beans and flour? Explain how their diet had changed. (Think about why people need "fast food.")

HUNTERS AND ANIMALS

The young man of the 1600s wonders why the animals and people of Mi'kma'kik are disappearing.

The beaver are disappearing. This winter the hunters have had to travel farther inland than ever to find them, and even then they are scarce. We're camping on the shore of a small lake with my father's brother. I miss the ocean — and the taste of fish.

Great-grandfather is staying on the coast this winter with his daughter and her family. They have some meat and fish stored there. Last fall, Great-grandfather put away some groundnuts and cranberries, too. When he was a young man, he used to stay on the coast all winter, fishing and seal hunting. Once in a while he and other men would go off for a few days to hunt. But there was always plenty of smoked meat and fish, moose fat, and nuts and berries to last through the winter.

Now we have to hunt all winter because this is when the furs are best. We depend on hunting for food, too, because we're so far from the coast. If the hunters catch nothing, we go hungry.

Sometimes I wonder why the animals and people are disappearing. When Great-grandfather was a boy, his mother told him that people got sick and died when they broke rules about hunting or cooking. Sometimes the power of a *puoin* could make a person die. I think the sickness comes from the Europeans now. Whenever a group of fishermen comes to

42

Mi'kma'kik, there is another sickness soon after.

The animals are still offended, though. Hunters just take the skins and leave the meat and bones to spoil, or use it as bait or food for dogs. The animals used to help people live, but now they won't give themselves up. The hunters and the animals don't know each other anymore.

1. What are *groundnuts*?
2. Why do you suppose hunters did things that would anger the animals?

WRITING:

1. The subject of your biography sees Europeans for the first time. Describe this incident, and tell what he or she thinks about the strange things the Europeans have. What does your subject think about the ways European people talk and act? This is the last chapter of your biography. Make up an ending that shows how a meeting with Europeans affects your subject. The ending might be happy or sad. (Whatever you include should be based on your reading in this and other books.)

or

2. What things did the Europeans have that would have surprised the Mi'kmaq? What kinds of things would have been familiar to them? Why? What kinds of things did the Mi'kmaq have that would have surprised Europeans? Why? List as many things as you can.

BEGINNING OF NEW WAYS

By the 1600s the coming of the Europeans had changed every part of Mi'kmaq life — where people lived, what they ate, what they believed, and how they worked together or even quarrelled among themselves. But even though the Europeans had been visiting Mi'kma'kik for almost 150 years, they had not yet found it necessary to settle there.

The Mi'kmaq were still the only people who really lived in Mi'kma'kik. They kept their own language and remembered the tales of their ancestors. At birth, at marriage, and at death, Mi'kmaq men and women continued to follow many of the old customs. Even if they were no longer close to the animals, they remained skilful hunters and fishermen. They were not entirely dependent on the Europeans, and could still make tools from stone and bone. They knew every stream and every portage, and they could travel swiftly by canoe or by foot. In this way, the Mi'kmaq knew what was happening throughout their land.

They had found a way to survive, and they adapted to the new conditions. The Mi'kmaq way of life changed, but it did not die.

Typical French soldiers who came to New France around 1660.

DID YOU KNOW?

It took 12 days to travel by canoe from Port Royal to Quebec City.

| 10 000 BC | 9000 BC | 8000 BC | 7000 BC | 6000 BC | 5000 BC | 4000 BC | 3000 BC | 2000 BC | 1000 BC | 0 | 1000 AD | 2000 AD |

ARE YOU CURIOUS?
1. Find out about the routes the Mi'kmaq used when travelling by canoe. How could they have travelled from Big Cove, New Brunswick, or Minas Basin, Nova Scotia, to Quebec? How did they travel from Cape Breton to Newfoundland?
2. Find out about the kinds of small boats the Europeans used in the fisheries. The Mi'kmaq quickly learned to use these boats and to put sails on their own canoes.
3. Why hadn't Europeans settled in Mi'kma'kik before 1600?
4. Why didn't the Mi'kmaq try to avoid contact with the Europeans, or make them leave Mi'kma'kik?
5. Did the Mi'kmaq gain anything from the Europeans? What do you think? What might a Mi'kmaq have thought in 1600?

THE FRENCH

By the end of the 1500s most of the Europeans fishing, trading, and preaching along the coasts of the Maritimes were French. In spite of the changes they had brought to Mi'kma'kik they were generally accepted by the Mi'kmaq, who welcomed their trade goods.

At the beginning of the 1600s, men and women from France began coming to live in Mi'kma'kik. The French wanted to build settlements there to show other countries — especially England — that France controlled the fishing grounds and shipping routes in the Gulf of St. Lawrence and the nearby Atlantic. In 1605, Samuel de Champlain and Sieur de Monts built the first French farming settlement at Port Royal. For the next 150 years, French officials in Paris encouraged settlers to go to Mi'kma'kik, which was the eastern part of the land they called "Acadia". Acadian settlers worked small farms near the shore. For cropland and pastures, they found it easier to drain saltwater marshes than to clear trees in the forests.

A few settlers traded with the Mi'kmaq for furs. The Mi'kmaq spent their summers near French settlements, where they could carry

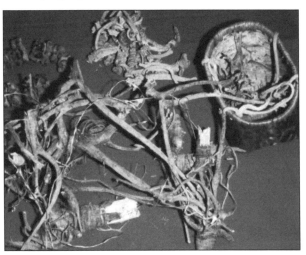
Pako'si (Flagroot) used to make traditional medicines.

on trade, moving away to hunt and trap during the winter. As the beaver disappeared, the demand for moose hides grew. But the main interest of the French government continued to be in fishing. *There were always more fishermen than settlers along the coasts of Acadia.*

EXPORTS FROM LOUISBOURG, 1753

EXPORTS	VALUE, IN LIVRES*
Fish & Fish products	1 213 716
Lumber & lumber products	87 204
Furs & hides	18 386

*Unit of money

A Spanish visitor to Louisbourg wrote: These natives were not absolutely subjects of the King of France, nor entirely independent of him. They acknowledged him lord of the country, but without any change in their way of living; or submitting themselves to his laws; and so far were they from paying any tribute, that they received annually from France a quantity of apparel, gunpowder, muskets, brandy, and several kinds to tools, in order to keep them quiet and attached to the French interest.

Juan y Antonio d'Ulloa, A Voyage to South America (translated by John Adams 2 vols. London 1806) II: 376-377.

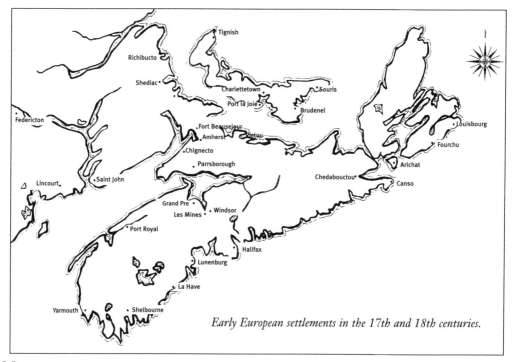

Early European settlements in the 17th and 18th centuries.

Make an imaginary map of a part of the coast of Mi'kma'kik where there was a French settlement. Show where the Mi'kmaq lived during each season. Also show places where the French and the Mi'kmaq fished. How does this map compare with the one you made earlier? Think about:
— where the "boundaries" of the Mi'kmaq community might have been;
— where different foods were found.

What was surprising to the Spanish visitor? Try to put his account into your own words.

ARE YOU CURIOUS?
Find out about Louisbourg, N.S. When did the French settle there? Why? Why is Louisbourg well known today?

THE FRENCH AND THE ENGLISH

Ever since the early years of exploration, England and France had been rivals for trade, fishing, and land in North America. They fought over Mi'kma'kik just as they fought over land in other parts of the continent. English settlers came to Mi'kma'kik, too.

English and French settlers had very different ways of living with the Mi'kmaq. When the French settled in Mi'kma'kik, they considered it French territory, not Mi'kmaq land. But they were willing to consider the Mi'kmaq citizens of France and let them live there. They travelled and worked among the Mi'kmaq and were friendly with *saqamaws*, *kinaps*, and *puoins*. They kept up this friendship by providing the Mi'kmaq with gifts and trade items at many trading posts. Some French settlers married Mi'kmaq women, and the couples spent time in both Mi'kmaq and Acadian communities.

The English tried to buy land from the Mi'kmaq, or — if that failed — to take it by force. Once they owned land, however, or obtained it from France by treaties, the English believed that no one else could live on it without their permission. But the Mi'kmaq believed they had given Europeans the right to use their land — *not to own it*. They saw no reason not to continue using it themselves, as they did where French

Typical blockhouse of an English fort reconstructed at St. Andrews, New Brunswick.

47

settlers lived. Because of this difference in understanding about territory and because the Mi'kmaq were close allies of the French, the English did not trust the Mi'kmaq and were afraid of them. Instead of trading and being friendly with the Mi'kmaq, the English government used its money to build forts and arm soldiers. In some places along the southern shore of Nova Scotia, English settlers even burned the forests to keep Mi'kmaq away from their settlements.

THE MI'KMAQ VS THE ENGLISH

The Mi'kmaq did not stand idly by while European settlers fought over their land: they took an active part in the struggle. By the 1740s, Mi'kmaq were deeply involved in the fighting between the French and the English in Nova Scotia. They wanted to protect their own right to use the land, to fish and hunt. They sided with the French, who helped to organize raids on English settlements. French priests, such as Antoine Maillard and Jean-Louis LeLoutre, worked closely with the Mi'kmaq, recruiting raiders.

The Mi'kmaq were skilful fighters not only on land, but on the sea as well. During the early 1700s, Mi'kmaq sailors captured at least 50 English fishing boats. Once a Mi'kmaq raiding party sailed all the way to Port-aux-Basques, Newfoundland, to capture a large schooner. The English sailors, frightened when they saw themselves surrounded, gave up the ship without much of a fight. The Mi'kmaq had the English crew sail the schooner back to Ile Royale (Cape Breton Island). But the Acadians there, who had to "Keep peace" with their English enemies, arranged — as they usually did— to have the crew released and the boat returned to its owners.

In response to the raids, the English, in 1744, brought Captain John Gorham and his "Rangers" to Nova Scotia to kill Mi'kmaq people. The English offered money for the scalps of Mi'kmaq men, women, and children. Mi'kmaq had to hide in the woods, where some of them built stockades to protect themselves.

It was no longer safe for them to stay near the coast for fishing or trading. In the past, many Mi'kmaq families had settled down near the Acadian settlements, at first just in the summertime, but eventually staying year-round. By the 1740s, trade with the Mi'kmaq was mainly for moose hides, which brought a good price in France. The fighting made it difficult — if not impossible — for the Mi'kmaq to continue trading. For 150 years, until a treaty was signed in 1763, the fighting between the French and English made life hard for the Mi'kmaq in Nova Scotia and New Brunswick. It started when the English attacked and burned Port Royal in 1613.

> *ARE YOU CURIOUS?*
>
> Read about the history of the Maritimes during the 1600s and 1700s.
>
> Make maps to show the boundaries of Acadia and Nova Scotia in 1605, 1632, 1667, 1713, and 1763.

| 10 000 BC | 9000 BC | 8000 BC | 7000 BC | 6000 BC | 5000 BC | 4000 BC | 3000 BC | 2000 BC | 1000 BC | 0 | 1000 AD | 2000 AD |

1. How would you describe the differences between what the French and the English thought about the Mi'kmaq?
2. Who do you think had a fairer attitude toward Mi'kmaq land — the French or the English? Or wouldn't you call either one "fair"?

The French vs The English in Nova Scotia — a Timeline

1605	The French settle at Port Royal.
1613	The English burn Port Royal.
1632	Treaty of St. Germain-en-Laye: the French get Acadia and Nova Scotia.
1632-1654	French settlers arrive in greater numbers.
1654-1670	The English patrol Bay of Fundy coasts to prevent Mi'kmaq and Acadian raids on New England.
1667	Treaty of Breda: the French get Acadia and Nova Scotia. The English give it up by 1670.
1710	The English recapture Port Royal. They rebuild it and name it Annapolis Royal.
1713	Treaty of Utrecht. The English get Nova Scotia. The French get Cape Breton (Île Royale) and build a fort at Louisbourg. English settlers come to the south shore of Nova Scotia; French settlers come to Île Royale and the Fundy shore.
1744	Captain John Gorham comes from Boston with his "Rangers".
1745	Father Maillard and Father LeLoutre are arrested by the English and set to England.
1749	English settlers come to Halifax. Maillard and LeLoutre return to Nova Scotia.
1755	The Acadians are expelled from Nova Scotia.
1758	The Acadians are expelled from Nova Scotia.
1758	The English destroy Louisbourg.
1763	Treaty of Paris. The English take control of Nova Scotia, Prince Edward Island, and Cape Breton Island. Acadian settlers begin to return in small numbers.

(Notice that all the Treaties were made in Europe.)

1. Why did the Mi'kmaq raid English settlements?
2. How did the wars between the French and the English affect Mi'kmaq communities? What might a map of a Mi'kmaq community in 1744 look like?

A LETTER FROM MONSIEUR DE LA VARENNE

On 8 May, 1756, Monsieur de la Varenne, a Frenchman living in Acadia, wrote a letter to a friend in Rochelle, France. In the letter he wrote that the main reason the Mi'kmaq were on good terms with the French was that the English treated the Mi'kmaq badly. The English gave them presents only when they needed their help right away in a fight against the French. It was clear to the Mi'kmaq, wrote de la Varenne, that they were being used. They didn't forget all the times the English had been rude to them or had cheated them — while the French were treating them well.

Monsieur de la Varenne wrote that French missionaries lived among the Mi'kmaq. They knew what the Mi'kmaq liked and they knew how to get along with them. The main reason that the Mi'kmaq liked the French — according to de la Varenne — was that they tried "to fall into the Mi'kmaq way of life, to adopt their manners, range the woods with them, and become as keen hunters as themselves." The Mi'kmaq liked having the French copy them, but, de la Varenne admitted, they (Mi'kmaq) were also adopting some French ways, such as "trafficking and bartering, and knowing the use of money of which they were before totally ignorant."

1. Why did the English have a hard time getting the Mi'kmaq on their side?

2. What were the French doing to keep the Mi'kmaq on their side?

3. Why do you think the Mi'kmaq were pleased to see the French imitating them, yet did not care to imitate the French?

From the title page of a translation of Pere Maillard's writing agout the Mi'kmaq and the Maliseets.

AN
ACCOUNT
OF THE
CUSTOMS and MANNERS
OF THE
MICMAKIS and MARICHEETS
Now Dependent on the
Government of CAPE-BRETON.

FROM
An Original FRENCH Manuscript-Letter,
Never Published,

Written by a FRENCH ABBOT,
Who resided many Years, in quality of Missionary, amongst them.

To which are annexed,
Several PIECES, relative to NOVA SCOTIA, and to NORTH-AMERICA in general.

LONDON:
Printed for S. HOOPER and A. MORLEY at Gay's-Head, near Beaufort-Buildings in the Strand. MDCCLVIII

A Letter from Edward Cornwallis to the Bishop of Quebec, Monseigneur Henri Marie du Breud de Pontbriand, 12 December, 1749.

Est-ce bien vous qui aves envoye Le Loutre pour missionnaire aux Mi'kmaq, est-ce pour leur bien que ce prestre excite ces miserables a exercer leur cruautes contre ceux qui leur fait toutes sortes d'amities, est-ce pour leur interet qu'il les empeche de s'unir a un peuple civilise et chretien, et de jouir de tous les avantages d'un doux Gouvernement. Si vous lui avez donne cette mission, je suis certain que vous ne luy aves pas ordonne de mener les (Mi'kmaq) a leur propre Ruine, et Contre les allies de son Roy.
(AC CHB 29:81v.)

| 10 000 BC | 9000 BC | 8000 BC | 7000 BC | 6000 BC | 5000 BC | 4000 BC | 3000 BC | 2000 BC | 1000 BC | 0 | 1000 AD | 2000 AD |

Is it really you who have sent LeLoutre as a missionary to the Mi'kmaq? Is it for their good that this priest incites them to practice their acts of cruelty against those who help them in so many ways? Is it in their interest that he prevents them from joining with a civilized and Christian people and enjoying all the benefits of a generous government? If you did give him this mission, I am certain that you did not order him to lead the Mi'kmaq to their very ruin, and against the allies of their ruler.
— Edward Cornwallis, founder of Halifax and Governor of Nova Scotia.

1. Why did Edward Cornwallis tell Monseigneur de Pontbriand that the English were trying to be friendly toward the Mi'kmaq? What does he want Monseigneur de Pontbriand to do?
2. Why were the Acadians in Nova Scotia British subjects in 1744? What about the Acadians in Île Royale?

THE LOYALISTS

When the English took full control of the Maritimes in 1763, life became more peaceful but the Mi'kmaq still faced hard times.

In the 1780s after the American Revolution, Loyalists from the United States came to the Maritimes in great numbers. The provinces became a centre for lumbering, fishing, and shipbuilding industries, which did well through the first half of the 1800s. The Mi'kmaq, however, did not share in the prosperity.

Before the Loyalists came, the Mi'kmaq had always managed to make their own living, But now the Loyalists wanted to settle along the rivers and estuaries to take advantage of the good farmland there. They cut timber, cleared the land, and killed moose and caribou. As a result, the Mi'kmaq could not keep up their old way of life. They were forced to wander over wider areas to find food.

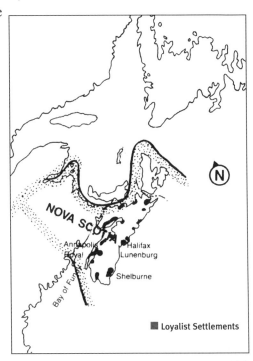

The extent of Nova Scotia before 1784, and Loyalist settlements.

Selections from Nova Scotia government documents about the Mi'kmaq*

They have no settled place of abode, but

ramble about in the woods and support themselves by hunting or fishing. Wherever they kill a moose, deer or caribou, they fix their tent, or as they call it wigwham, and continue as long as they can find any game near the place. After which they remove their quarters in quest of fresh game. They are very expert in hunting, and excellent marksmen with the gun. (Robinson and Rispin, Journey through Nova Scotia. York: C. Etherington, 1774)

*Some government accounts of Mi'kmaq life in the 1800s. Journal of the Legislative Assem. S. Report on Indian Affairs for 1843; Legislative Assembly of N.S. Journals 1843: appendix I 1848a: appendix 2, Annual Reports of the Department of Indian Affairs: 1882, 1883.

The condition of the Indians would not be so bad could they find in the forests of Nova Scotia the same food and fur as formerly, but the sound of the settler's ax has scared away the moose, the caribou, the bear, the beaver, the fox, and the martin, and (the ax's) edge, together with the fire, by destroying their haunts and retreats, has greatly reduced their numbers... The supply of necessaries of life which the Indians derive from the making of baskets is at all times scanty, uncertain, and insufficient and has lately become more so in consequence of the scarcity of fuel in the vicinity of Halifax, which has compelled the Indians to remove into the country during the winter where they do not find Sale for their work. (1820s)

It is to be regretted that so little judgment has been exercised in the selection of

Mi'kmaq figure studies by Mary Chaplin, 1839.

them (In regard to Native lands) — the same quantity, if reserved in spots where the soil is good, on navigable streams, or in places where fish was abundant, and game within reach, would now be a valuable resource. All the land reserved in the County (Halifax) is sterile and comparatively valueless. In Yarmouth, Hants, Colchester, Pictou, and Guysborough, there are no reserves,...in... Dartmouth and Halifax they have no lands. (1843)

I cannot close this Report, without again reminding you of the necessity of immediately procuring the Indians of this County a piece of Land on the Tide Waters, to operate upon. At present they are driven from place to place, without a resting place for their feet — their game is gone — firewood is denied them, and the very sanctuaries of their dead, are in some instances desecrated and ploughed over. (1843)

The erection of dams across the rivers has destroyed some of the best salmon and alewife fisheries in the Province. The best shore fisheries are occupied by the white inhabitants, from which the Indian is sometimes driven by force... Herds of swine have consumed the shell-fish upon the shores. (1848)

The timber they require for their handiwork is becoming very scarce. The Indians settled near Kentville, having to travel some fifteen miles (24 km) to procure the more valuable kinds and even the young maples, from which the females make the baskets and fancy work, are cut and drawn, or in many instances lugged home on their backs a distance of from three to five miles (5 - 8 km). (1882)

It is impossible to form any accurate estimate of the proceeds of their coopering and basket-work, as they barter these away in most cases in small lots for the necessaries of life during the course of the year. Thus the agent is always at a loss how to value the proceeds of those works, he can only make an approximate guess of their value. (1883)

James Dawson

In Nova Scotia officials encouraged the Mi'kmaq to settle down, and not move about from season to season. Some Mi'kmaq obtained grants of land and took up farming.

A few Mi'kmaq farms were successful and continued to be productive up until the 1950s. Other Mi'kmaq tried their hand at making shingles, barrels, casks, baskets, and other farm supplies.

They sold beautiful quillwork. But the Loyalists had come to Nova Scotia with very little money to spend on such items. Many Mi'kmaq had to continue to more from place to place, hunting, fishing, and doing odd jobs when possible, in order to get by.

MI'KMAQ CRAFT ITEMS FROM THE LATE 1800S AND EARLY 1900S

Household items: butter-tubs and wash-tubs, churns and buckets
Industrial items: ax and pick-handles, peavey sticks, barrels, mast-hoops
Sports Items: canoes, snowshoes, paddles and oars, hockey sticks
Fancy Work: decorative baskets, eyeglass cases, moccasins, etc. (made by women and older men)

1. Why didn't the Mi'kmaq share in Maritime prosperity?
2. What kinds of farms did the Loyalists have?
3. Why did Nova Scotia officials want the Mi'kmaq to settle down, and not move from place to place?

WRITING:

It is 1800. Your class is a group of Mi'kmaq people who have lived together for a long time. The area where you usually hunt and fish can no longer support you, and you must decide what to do. New Brunswick officials have offered your group a tract of land to farm; and you have to decide whether or not you will accept it. As a class, decide what to do. Then write a letter to the Governor of the province.

A stamp showing traditional crafts.

Pictures of a few articles made by Mi'kmaq craft workers. What articles can you identify in the pictures?

MI'KMAQ LAND

In 1763 a Royal Proclamation stated that all land which had not been purchased by the Crown was reserved to the Indians for hunting and fishing — unless the Crown itself purchased land. No private individual could buy Indian land, and anyone who had settled on Indian land had to move. The Proclamation applied to all of Nova Scotia (which included New Brunswick at that time). Little was done to make it work. From the time of the Proclamation to this day, the Mi'kmaq have never negotiated with the Crown or signed a treaty to give up land or hunting and fishing rights. Today they claim these rights as they were set out over 200 years ago.

Government officials ignored the Proclamation. They felt that they could decide where the Mi'kmaq should live.

During the late 1700s and early 1800s, they "gave" Mi'kmaq individual, families, and communities the right to occupy certain tracts of land. Eventually many of these tracts became recognized by law as Indian Reserves, set aside for the use of the

Mi'kmaq communities in the Maritimes, Gaspé and Newfoundland.

Mi'kmaq only. But settlers kept using the land on the edges of the reserves for farming or cutting timber. Although these activities were illegal, the provinces made few serious attempts to stop them. In fact the government sometimes took away reserve land by law, saying, as in the New Brunswick Indian Reserves Act of 1884, that extensive tracts of valuable Land reserved for the Indians in various parts of this Province tend greatly to retard the settlement of the Country, while large portions of them are not, in their present neglected state, productive of any benefit to the people for whose use they were reserved.... It is desirable that these Lands should be put upon a footing as to render them not only beneficial to the Indians but conducive to the settlement of the Country.

Although many plans were made to have them settle down in permanent communities, most Mi'kmaq resisted. The government said it would help farmers get started and protect Mi'kmaq land. But the Mi'kmaq saw that the government was unable — or unwilling— to keep its promises.

Confederation in 1867 (1873 in Prince Edward Island) meant little change for the Mi'kmaq. They had learned by then that the best way to keep their own communities together, and to keep their language and customs alive, was to have a little to do with the government as possible. They simply continued living as independently as they could. Some did settle down, other continued a wandering life — working here and there. This way of life went on largely unchanged until the 1940s.

1. How could government officials "give" the Mi'kmaq land?
2. Do you think it is fair for the Mi'kmaq still to claim land rights in New Brunswick and Nova Scotia? What questions would help you decide whether it is fair or not?
3. Why did the Mi'kmaq think it best to ignore the government's plans? Why did they feel it was important to keep separate from non-Mi'kmaq communities?
4. How would a Mi'kmaq community in 1840 have been different from a community in 1440? In what ways might it have been the same? Think about:
   — the "boundaries" of the community
   — finding or raising of food
   — where people live in each season
   — travelling to other Mi'kmaq communities
5. What might have been the duties of a *saqamaw* in 1840?

Think about what Mi'kmaq men and women did for work in the 1400s. How might this have changed by the 1800s? Make a new chart of your ideas about men's work and women's work.

SOMETHING OLD, SOMETHING NEW

Sometimes traditional activities help modern industries. In the late 1800s, Mi'kmaq men from a reserve near Digby, Nova Scotia, hunted porpoises in the Bay of Fundy. Farmers in the Annapolis Valley area used the oil from the porpoises to lubricate their equipment. In the 1890s when better grease and oil was made from petroleum, farmers no longer needed porpoise oil. The Mi'kmaq fishermen went out of business.

In what other ways did Mi'kmaq use oldtime skills to help modern industries?

TREATY RIGHTS

People's rights which are affirmed in a treaty are called treaty rights. The Mi'kmaq and Maliseet nations have treaty rights. They are the original inhabitants of the Maritimes. When the British asserted their authority over the region in the 1700s, the Mi'kmaq and Maliseet lived there. They began to sign treaties of peace and friendship with the British in 1725. They never signed any treaty in which they gave up land, and they never gave up their right to hunt and fish. The first treaty was designed to establish a long-lasting peace. It also affirmed the Native peoples' right to hunt and fish. Even though fighting broke out from time to time after 1725, and even though the Mi'kmaq and the Maliseet lost control of most of their land, they continued to sign treaties of peace and friendship with the British. Important ones were signed in 1760 and 1761. Then, in the 1770s, Loyalists and other settlers began to arrive in the Maritimes in large numbers. The treaties were still valid, but from that time on the British government ignored them. After Confederation, the Canadian government continued to ignore the treaties. However, in 1999, the Supreme Court of Canada ruled that the Mi'kmaq and the Maliseet still have the right to hunt and fish freely.

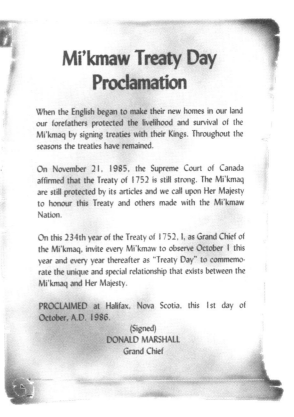

Mi'kmaw Treaty Day Proclamation

When the English began to make their new homes in our land our forefathers protected the livelihood and survival of the Mi'kmaq by signing treaties with their Kings. Throughout the seasons the treaties have remained.

On November 21, 1985, the Supreme Court of Canada affirmed that the Treaty of 1752 is still strong. The Mi'kmaq are still protected by its articles and we call upon Her Majesty to honour this Treaty and others made with the Mi'kmaw Nation.

On this 234th year of the Treaty of 1752, I, as Grand Chief of the Mi'kmaq, invite every Mi'kmaw to observe October 1 this year and every year thereafter as "Treaty Day" to commemorate the unique and special relationship that exists between the Mi'kmaq and Her Majesty.

PROCLAIMED at Halifax, Nova Scotia, this 1st day of October, A.D. 1986.

(Signed)
DONALD MARSHALL
Grand Chief

Rita Joe, Mi'kmaq poet, of Eskasoni, Nova Scotia.

When I was small
I used to help my father
Make axe handles.
Coming home from the wood with a bundle
Of *maskwi, snawey, aqamoq,**
My father would chip away,
Carving with a crooked knife,
Until a well-made handle appeared,
Ready to be sand-papered
By my brother.

When it was finished
We started another,
Sometimes working through the night
With me holding a lighted shaving
To light their way
When our kerosene lamp ran dry.

Then in the morning
My mother would be happy
That there would be food today
When my father sold our work.

Rita Joe.

paper birch, rock maple, white ash

THE 1940s

In Nova Scotia, during the 1940s, the Mi'kmaq learned that they could not continue to ignore the government. The Department of Indian Affairs decided to move all the Mi'kmaq in the province to two reserves, Eskasoni (ess-k'-ZOH-nee) on Cape Breton Island and Shubenacadie (shoo-b'-NAG-a-dee) on the mainland. They were told they would have new homes with barns and farm equipment, or that they could have jobs in new businesses that would be started near the reserves. There would be better schools and modern conveniences — electricity, running water, and sewers.

Some Mi'kmaq people accepted these offers, others did not. A Mi'kmaq woman tells why she and her family moved to Eskasoni but later returned to their home community, Whycocomagh (why-KAH-g'mah).

MOVING DAY

Do you know why they want to move all the Mi'kmaq in Cape Breton to Eskasoni? I do. They tell us it will be better for us — more jobs and better houses. But really it's to make things easier for the Indian Affairs people. They won't have to travel around from reserve to reserve, and there will be fewer schools and offices to pay for.

We moved away to Eskasoni — not because we believed what they said about new jobs and farms. After all we already had our own farm at Whycocomagh, and we were doing quite well. We had a few dairy cows, some pigs and sheep, and a small apple orchard. I made baskets, and my husband did some woodwork and carpentry. We sold some of our products.

No, we went to Eskasoni because we thought we had to. A man from Indian Affairs told us there would be no more school at our reserve, no medical services, no relief payments. He said that people who didn't move to Eskasoni wouldn't even be counted as Mi'kmaq any more. My husband had served in the Armed Forces during World War II, but he said we couldn't get the money and new house we were supposed to have unless we went to Eskasoni. None of this turned out to be true as we found out later. We almost decided not to go; but when my father-in-law said he was going to move, we went with him.

It was sad to leave our farm in the early spring, especially knowing that no one would live there after us. We took as much of our furniture as we could, but we had to sell all the animals. When we first got to Eskasoni, we stayed with a cousin until we could get a house of our own. It was very hard for my cousin. He had to take in a few other relatives, too. The land that he and his neighbours were farming was being divided up for the newcomers to live on. No wonder there were hard feelings!

Once the new houses were built, there were no jobs. The farm plot we were supposed to have was too far from our house. The soil was poor. When we'd been at Eskasoni almost a year — it was the following spring — one of my sons got into a bad fight with a boy from another reserve. That was the last straw. I decided we had all had enough. Come what may, we'd go back to Whycocomagh.

We were all so happy to leave Eskasoni that we didn't care that we might have no way to get our old farm going again. We really didn't know what to expect. It had been sad to leave our old farm in the first place, but the return seemed even worse. The house stood there with broken windows and a sagging door. Our barn roof had broken through and the yard was all grown up. My brother and his family, who had never left our reserve, helped us settle in as best we could.

The farm was never the same again. We had a garden, but we didn't have enough money to raise animals. Some of the orchard had been cut down for firewood while we were away. Because a lot of people who'd moved to Eskasoni stayed there, there weren't as many people living at Whycocomagh any more, so we didn't have as many customers. But I'm glad we came back. It was the best thing for all of us. My sister and her family did stay at Eskasoni. There weren't any jobs closer than Sydney, and that was too far away for her husband to travel without a car. They finally got a little house, but for years they've had a hard time making a living.

In 1953, because so many Mi'kmaq had refused to cooperate, Indian Affairs gave up trying to move people to Eskasoni and Shubenacadie. But even so, these two reserves had become very large. More than half of all the other reserves in Nova Scotia were now empty.

An early photograph (1930's) of children attending Residential School.

1. Why do you think the Department of Indian Affairs decided to move all the Mi'kmaq in Nova Scotia to two reserves?
2. Compare Moving Day in the 1940s with the young woman's account of Moving Day five hundred years earlier (pp 22-23). Why did each of these two women move? What did each one look forward to? Did they each have something to regret?

ARE YOU CURIOUS
Investigate residential school experiences in your own area by reading (see the booklist on pages 71-72) or by interviewing former students. How were experiences in the residential schools different for different people?

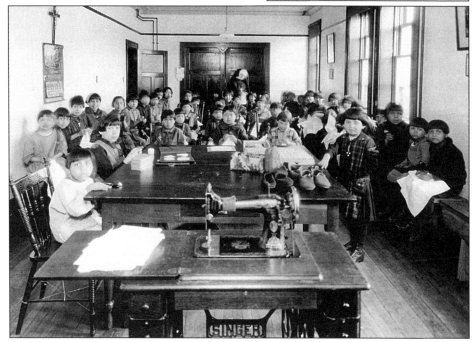

Class of Mi'kmaq girls taken in the Shubenacadie Residential School, Shubenacadie, NS, 1929

61

MI'KMAQ TODAY

During the past fifty years great changes have taken place in Mi'kmaq communities. Many Mi'kmaq left the reserves in the 1950s and 1960s to find jobs. For some this meant moving to Halifax or Fredericton — or to Boston, Montreal, or farther west. Today, most of the Native people who live in Boston are Mi'kmaq.

The communities began to look different from the way they had in the 1940s and 1950s, when indoor plumbing and even electric power were rare, and when jobs were few and wages low. Mi'kmaq people no longer ignore the government. They are taking an active part in planning improvements in the communities. There are new jobs and new Mi'kmaq run businesses. Mi'kmaq have more control over their schools and government operations in their communities. In the 1970s, for the first time, large numbers of Mi'kmaq men and women began to attend universities and trade schools. Mi'kmaq licensed teachers return to their communities or nearby provincial schools to teach Mi'kmaq children. There are still problems. Unemployment is always high and many children do not finish high school. In many communities there were no schools at all until the early 1980s. When schools were set up, they were run by the Church or the Government. Mi'kmaq parents and community members had no say in how their children were taught or how school money was spent. There were no Mi'kmaq school committees.

As children went to school, they were often confused by the unfamiliar standards of behaviour. The strict school routine, with its rules and punishments and ideas of what was rude — such as calling an adult by his or her first name — made most children want to stay home. Teachers did not speak Mi'kmaq. At some schools, children were strapped for speaking their own language.

At home, children's education was different. Their parents expected them to make their own decisions about what to do. They learned how to behave and how to make a living by

Kids are always welcome at MMI! (l-r) Paige Frost, Jade Frost, Angel Bernard, and Kendra Frost pose with Helen Bernard.

| 10 000 | 9000 BC | 8000 BC | 7000 BC | 6000 BC | 5000 BC | 4000 BC | 3000 BC | 2000 BC | 1000 BC | 0 | 1000 AD | 2000 AD |

following the examples of the men and women they spent time with. Children worked with adults at adult tasks, learning to make things for sale, to find their way through woods and waterways, to read prayers and sing hymns, to provide food for their families. At school there were no adult activities; everything was planned for children. They felt cut off from their parents and the life of their communities.

Today, Mi'kmaq teachers and principals and other community members interested in schooling are planning studies that are suited to Mi'kmaq ways of learning. They encourage children to be proud of their Mi'kmaq heritage. At the school at Eskasoni, in Nova Scotia, children learn about Mi'kmaq history and traditional beliefs. They study these in Mi'kmaq and in English, so that they are able to learn from both oral tradition and written records. In New Brunswick, there are Mi'kmaq-language teachers at almost every grade school attended by Mi'kmaq children. These teachers believe that it is important for children to keep their language, so that they will know more about their parents and grandparents — who have spoken Mi'kmaq all their lives — and so that they can continue to be part of the

Barbara Clement has just sung O Canada in Mi'kmaq and Maliseet at the UNB Encaenia, May 1999.

1999 Graduates, Barbara Brown (St. Mary's), Helen Bernard (Gesgapegiag and Red Bank), Barbara Clement (Big Cove) and Holly Bernard (Eskasoni).

Mi'kmaq community.

Many parents and teachers do not want to push children to leave their community in order to make a living. Instead, they want them to know things that can be or practical value to themselves and to their people. The Mi'kmaq need lawyers, social workers, doctors, teachers, builders, and business people. Even if they cannot find jobs there, young men and women will still be part of the community. As one Mi'kmaq father tells his children, "Don't count on working here, but don't forget the community."

In Quebec, New Brunswick, Nova Scotia, and Prince Edward Island Mi'kmaq have taken control of their own schools. Mi'kmaq school committees, parents, and teachers work together to run them. Children in all the Maritime Provinces can study Mi'kmaq history, learn about traditional government and geography, read and write the Mi'kmaq language, and learn to make baskets, quillwork, and carvings — along with a full programme of English language studies. More students are staying in school to graduate. But they still look forward to summertime, when they can spend their time with family and friends.

1. Why is it important that Mi'kmaq children study Mi'kmaq language and the history of Mi'kmaq people in school?
2. Imagine that you are going to start a school for Mi'kmaq children that will prepare them to work in their communities when they graduate. What should they know?
3. Tell how you would run the school so that the students are not separately grouped as children, but might work alongside adults, as Mi'kmaq children do at home today.

SUMMER HOLIDAYS

Every summer there are special occasions when Mi'kmaq people from different reserves get together. A Mi'kmaq girl from New Brunswick tells about her summer holidays.

My favourite day of the whole year is St. Anne's Day. Sometimes we go to Ste. Anne-de-Beaupré, in Quebec, but usually we spend that week at Chapel Island, near St. Peter's, Nova Scotia. That's where my mother went every summer before she was married to my dad - and moved here to Big Cove. My grandmother says that Mi'kmaq people have been gathering at Chapel Island every summer for hundreds of years. She showed me a big circle worn down in the dirt where people used to dance. Even before the first church was built — and Mi'kmaq weren't Catholic yet — they went there. Maybe that's why there seems to be a special feeling about Chapel Island.

My grandmother told me about the first priest who preached there — in 1757. His name was Father Maillard, and he was the one who built the first church. There was a wooden statue of St. Anne in it that had been brought all the way from France. My grandmother says this statue must have been very special because even though the church burned down seven times — mostly from lightning, but once from an English attack — the statue always survived. This is, it did until the last fire, in 1976, when it burned too. Now, there's a small, new church there, and lots of little cabins where people stay during the week of St. Anne's Day. Ours is painted blue. My grandfather built it for our family.

Why do I like going to Chapel Island? It's really a good feeling to be in a place where I feel close to all my ancestors. Grandma says she feels close to God there. She always gets there before us and fixes up the cabin with mattresses on the floor. She brings a lot of food, too. As soon as we got out of the boat last year, I ran up to see her. She took me around to see her relatives. I met two of her cousins who don't even live on a reserve — one was from Halifax and one was from Newfoundland. They seemed really serious — as

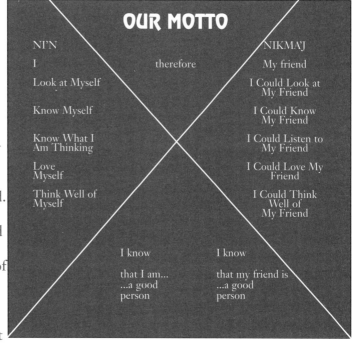

OUR MOTTO

NI'N		NIKMA'J
I	therefore	My friend
Look at Myself		I Could Look at My Friend
Know Myself		I Could Know My Friend
Know What I Am Thinking		I Could Listen to My Friend
Love Myself		I Could Love My Friend
Think Well of Myself		I Could Think Well of My Friend

I know that I am... ...a good person

I know that my friend is ...a good person

Procession of St. Anne in Chapel Island.

if coming to Chapel Island made them sad. My grandmother said they hadn't been there since they were my age. I stayed up late every night with my friends or listening to my grandparents telling stories.

Last year my grandmother and I watched the procession together. The important chiefs and council members looked so dignified with their banners and sashes. The priests wore their fanciest vestments. My grandmother told me that the chiefs used to be elected at Chapel Island. People would get married there and also settle their fights there. It was as if the Island were the centre of Mi'kma'kik — at least in Nova Scotia.

Nowadays a lot of my friends at Big Cove go to Ste. Anne-de-Beaupré. I went there two years ago with my aunt and uncle. They go every year. I like Ste. Anne-de-Beaupré because I get to see so many different people — not just Mi'kmaq, but other people from Canada and the United States. There's a special feeling there, too. People have bene healed there. I saw all the crutches that have been thrown away. We stayed at a campground with a lot of other Mi'kmaq people and it was exciting, like being at Chapel Island. My grandmother says that even in the old days Mi'kmaq people used to travel together to special places, and they always had a wonderful time.

BLUEBERRY RAKING

I bet I'll earn $300 in Maine this August. That'll be the most I've ever made. The first summer I went blueberry-raking I was only four years old — that was in 1976 — and I made $6.50. My mother let me help her fill up the boxes, but I think I ate more than I picked. The next year she bought me my own rake. Now I have my own place in the blueberries to rake, and I might make enough money for my school clothes. Maybe I can get a new bike too. I'll have to earn the money myself.

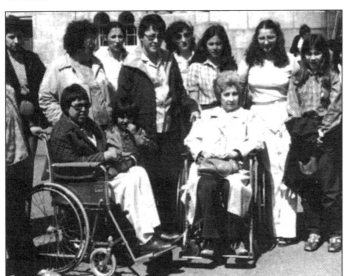

Many Mi'kmaq go to Ste. Anne-de-Beaupré in Quebec, for the feast of St. Anne.

My uncle's taking us to Maine in his big old van again. It always seems as if it's packed with about twenty people and piled up with suitcases on top. When we get there, we'll stay in the cabins out on the blueberry barrens. My grandmother

| 10 000 | 9000 BC | 8000 BC | 7000 BC | 6000 BC | 5000 BC | 4000 BC | 3000 BC | 2000 BC | 1000 BC | 0 | 1000 AD | 2000 AD |

says it's like the community, when she was a girl. No one speaks English. People sit around at night and tell stories. Sometimes we sing Mi'kmaq songs and dance. Everyone cooks outdoors. It's kind of a holiday, even though the work is very hard.

When my dad was little, he and his family really counted on the money they earned raking blueberries and picking potatoes — that's up in northern Maine — to help them live through the winter. They weren't paid very well, though, and sometimes they had to pick in places that other people had already raked. Now Passamaquoddy people from Maine own the blueberry land where we pick. They've promised to give us fairer pay. As a boy, Dad had to miss all of September in school to pick potatoes. Nowadays I think some people go to Maine as much for a holiday as for the money. My dad has a job in construction and my mom teaches school.

BASEBALL AND HOCKEY

The other thing I really like about summer is playing baseball. There are lots of teams in our community — from little kids to old timers. You should see my grandfather's team: they really know how to play ball! The teams play around the province, and we also play teams from the towns near us. It's fun to talk about baseball in Mi'kmaq while we're playing!

This summer my brother went to hockey camp. Next winter he'll be playing with the older boys. Actually, there are more hockey teams than baseball teams where I'm from. We have a rink, and every team has its own equipment. My mother sews the uniforms for my father's team. Hockey players travel a lot, some as far as Cape Breton Island.

I love those trips because there's always a big welcome at the other reserves. My mother tells us Mi'kmaq stories in the car as we're travelling along, and we always have big suppers when we arrive — just the way we do when we go to St. Anne's Day or to Maine. I learn a lot from travelling, and I don't think I'll ever get tired of it.

1. Why are Ste. Anne-de-Beaupré and Chapel Island important to Mi'kmaq people?
2. Why do you think travelling is important?
3. Compare this young girl's trips with the travels of the young man who loved feasts (pp.27-30). What did each one learn in his travels. In what ways are their lives the same?

TODAY IN MI'KMA'KIK

Mi'kmaq still travel and visit one another in the same places their ancestors visited hundreds of years ago. Staying in touch keeps alive some of the old traditions, the Mi'kmaq language, and the closeness of Mi'kmaq communities. Today, people are becoming more and more familiar with computers and modern medicine, with jet travel and big-city living, with the legal and political issues that affect their lives. At the same time, Mi'kmaq are moving back to Mi'kma'kik. Some like to spend their summer days in the uninhabited places of Mi'kma'kik. They go with their families to Malagawatch on the Bras d'Or Lakes or to the outer islands at the Lennox Island Reserve on Prince Edward Island — to camp and fish and live a little closer to the land they know so well. Mi'kma'kik will always be home for the Mi'kmaq.

> ## ARE YOU CURIOUS
> Find out about St. Anne. Who was she? Why is she the "patron saint" of many Native people in eastern Canada?

Ai! Mu knu'kaqann,
Mu nuji-wi'kikaqann,
Mu weskitaqawikasinukl kisna
    mikekni-napuikasinukl
Kekinua'tuenukl wlakue'l
    pa'qalaiwaqann.

Ta'n teluji-mtua'lukwi'tij nuji-
    kina'mua'tijik a.

Ke' kwilmi'tij,
Maqamikewe'l wisunn,
Apaqte'l wisunn,
Sipu'l;
Mukk kasa'tu mikuite'mmaqanmk
Wula knu'kaqann.

Ki' kelu'lk nemitmikl
Kmtne'l samqwann nisitk,
Kesikawitkl sipu'l.
Wula na kis-napui'kmu'kl
Mikuite'tmaqanminaq.
Nuji-kina'masultioq,
    we'jitutoqsip ta'n kisite'tmekl
Wisunn aqq ta'n pa'qi-klu'lk,
Tepqatmi'tij Lnu weja'tekemk
    weji-nsituita'timk.

Aye! no monuments,
No literature,
No scrolls or canvas-drawn pictures
Relate the wonders of our yesterday.

How frustrated the searchings
    of the educators.

Let them find
Land names,
Titles of seas,
Rivers;
Wipe them not from memory.
These are our monuments.

Breathtaking views —
Waterfalls on a mountain,
Fast flowing rivers.
These are our sketches
Committed to our memory.
Scholars, you fill find our art
In names and scenery,
Betrothed to the Indian
    since time began.

Rita Joe
Eskasoni, N. S.

PHOTO AND PRINT CREDITS

Micmac-Maliseet Institute, UNB 3
National Museum of Canada 19 (J-4174)
Nova Scotia Museum 25 (N-8467)
Ontario Department of Lands & Forests 42
Parks Canada 6 (CBH-183)
Public Archives Canada 26 (C-3689), 37 (C-42063), 38 (C-3686)
Rob Blanchard, UNB Audio Visual Services 62, 63
Royal Ontario Museum 52 (73166)
Mi'kmaq Maliseet Nations News 45, 65
Clayton Paul/Mi'kmaq Maliseet Nations News 58
Elsie Charles Basque 60
National Archives of Canada 61 (PA-185530)

Drawings are based on several sources, including CBC Halifax series of films on Mi'kmaq life (advisors Ruth H. Whitehead and Harold F. McGee, Nova Scotia Department of Education, Nova Scotia Media Services and Mi'kmaq Association for Cultural Studies) and The Mi'kmaq by Ruth H. Whitehead and Harold F. McGee.

Thanks to the Mi'maq Maliseet Nations News for its loan of photographs.

GLOSSARY

accumulation — collection
Algonquian — belonging to a group of Native peoples of northeastern North America
ancestor — people of one's own family or nation who lived long ago
aqamaw — (AH-h'm-ow) — white ash (tree)
archaeologist — one who searches for objects from the distant past

barrens — treeless land with poor soil
beaver lodge — beaver's home
bias — opinion that deeps one from thinking fairly
burial mound — low hill constructed by people for use as a cemetery

carcass — dead body of an animal
coopering — trade of making wooden barrels or tubs
cycle — a repeating set of changes, as in the seasons of the year

desecrated — treated something special (sacred) without respect
dewclaws — useless toe on foot of moose, deer, etc.
disabuse — free someone from wrong ideas or practices

elder — one of the respected older people in a community
environment — the earth, water, plants, and weather that surround a person or place
Epekwitk — (eh-BEH-gweetk) — Prince Edward Island
epidemic — rapid spread of a disease through a large group of people
estuary — broad mouth of a river, into which the tide flows

flexible — easily bent

glacier — broad sheet of ice covering many hectares of land
gouge — sharp tool used for carving

gunwales (GUN-'ls) — top edges of a canoe or small boat

harpoon — arrow or spear attached by a line to the hunter to pull in the large fish or sea mammal that has been caught
hearth — place for building a fire

immunity — freedom from or defence against a disease
Indian hemp — plant with a tough bark that can be split into twine for tying or binding
Iroquoian — belonging to a group of Native peoples living mainly in Quebec, Ontario, and New York State.

jikmaqan — (JEE-g'm-ah-'n) — rattle made of folded bark

keskmsit — (gess-K'M'-zeed) — extraordinary personal power
kinap — (GEE-nahb) — person with special powers
kwi's — (gweez) — son

league — old measure of distance, about 5 km
leister — fish-spear with prongs that keep the fish from slipping off the point

marrow — soft tissue from the inside of most bones
maskwi — (MAHS-kwee) — paper birch
migrate — move as a group to live in another land
Mi'kma'kik — (meeg-MAH-geeg) — homeland of the Mi'kmaq

oral traditions — stories of the past life of a group that have been passed from parents to children for many years

Paleo-Indians — a term archaeologists use for Native people who lived many thousands of years ago
pelt — animal skin with fur still on it

procession — usually a religious parade; line of people moving along
puoin — (boo-OH-een) — person with special powers

quillwork — decoration made with porcupine quills

reserve — land set aside for the use of a certain group of people
rival — someone trying to get the same thing that someone else wants or needs
rush mat — mat made of tough grasses woven together

saqamaw — (SAH-h'm-ow) — highly respected person in the community
site — place where people have lived or where something has been found
snawey — (s'NAH-way) — rock maple

territory — land that belongs to a group of people, or that is their home
thwart — cross bar of a canoe
tidal flat — land uncovered when the tide goes out
tundra — level, treeless plain in the Arctic region

Unama'kik — (OON-ah-mah-geeg) — Cape Breton Island
utensils — objects used for cooking or preparing food

vestments — clothes worn by a priest, minister, or other religious leader during a ceremony

watershed — region drained by one river system
waw — (wow) — egg
weir — trap, built like a fence, for catching fish in shallow water
wikuom — (WEEG-oo-ohm) — house or shelter of poles covered by bark, skins, or rush mats

BOOKLIST — WITH NOTES

Edwin T. Adney and Howard I. Chapelle
THE BARK CANOES AND SKIN BOATS OF NORTH AMERICA
Washington, D.C., Smithsonian Institution, 1964
    Sections on canoe construction and Mi'kmaq canoes; illustrations

Patricia M. Allen
METEPENAGIAG: NEW BRUNSWICK'S OLDEST VILLAGE
Fredericton, Goose Lane, 1994
    Early history of the Mi'kmaq of the Miramichi, as known from archaeological evidence and oral tradition; illustrated with original paintings by Roger Simon, Mi'kmaq artist, of Big Cove, N.B.

American Friends Service Committee
THE WABANAKIS OF MAINE AND THE MARITIMES
Bath, Maine, Maine Indian Program, 1989
    Excellent teacher resource, including many sections on the Mi'kmaq of the US and Canada

Alfred G. Bailey
THE CONFLICT OF EUROPEAN AND EASTERN ALGONKIAN CULTURES 1504-1700
(Second edition)
Toronto, University of Toronto Press, 1969
    The effects of contact on both the Native peoples and the Europeans

Michael J. Caduto and Joseph Bruchac
KEEPERS OF THE EARTH: NATIVE STORIES AND ENVIRONMENTAL ACTIVITIES FOR CHILDREN
Saskatoon, Fifth House Publishers, 1989
    Contains a number of Kluskap legends; see also other "Keepers" books in this series

J. Richard McEwan
MEMORIES OF A MI'KMAQ LIFE
Fredericton, Mi'kmaq-Maliseet Institute, 1988
    Life of a Mi'kmaq man from Bear River N.S., in the community and beyond

W.D. Hamilton and W.A. Spray
SOURCE MATERIALS RELATING TO THE NEW BRUNSWICK INDIAN
Fredericton, Hamray Books, 1977
    Primary-source documents about the Native peoples of New Brunswick, from Cartier's visit to Chaleur Bay in 1534 to Indian land sales in the 1860s

Rita Joe
POEMS OF RITA JOE (Halifax, N.S., Abanaki Press, 1978), **SONG OF ESKASONI: MORE POEMS OF RITA JOE** (Charlottetown, Ragweed Press, 1988), **LNU AND INDIAN WE'RE CALLED** (Charlottetown, P.E.I., Ragweed, 1991)
    Poetry by the best known Mi'kmaq poet

Rita Joe
SONG OF RITA JOE, AUTOBIOGRAPHY OF A MI'KMAQ POET
Charlottetown, Ragweed Press, 1996

Rita Joe and Lesley Choyce, editors
THE MI'KMAQ ANTHOLOGY
Lawrencetown, N.S., Pottersfield, 1997
    Writings by a number of contemporary Mi'kmaq authors

Isabelle Knockwood
OUT OF THE DEPTHS: THE EXPERIENCES OF MI'KMAQ CHILDREN AT THE INDIAN RESIDENTIAL SCHOOL AT SCHUBENACADIE, NOVA SCOTIA
Lockeport, N.S., Roseway, 1992
    Based on interviews with men and women who attended the residential school as children

Robert M. Leavitt
MALISEET & MI'KMAQ: FIRST NATIONS OF THE MARITIMES
Fredericton, New Ireland Press, 1995
    Sections on language, spirituality, arts, ancient times, land issues, and government

Charles A. Martijn
LES MI'KMAQ ET LA MER
Montreal, Recherches amerindiennes au Quebec, 1986
    History of the seafaring Mi'kmaq, including their presence on the Magdalene Islands and in Newfoundland; extensive bibliography

MI'KMAQ-MALISEET NATIONS NEWS (monthly newspaper) Truro, N.S., Mi'kmaq-Maliseet Nations News Association
    For subscription information: P.O. Box 1590, Truro, N.S. B2N 5V3

Lewis Mitchell; edited by Robert M. Leavitt and David A. Francis
WAPAPI AKONUTOMAKONOL / THE WAMPUM RECORDS: WABANAKI TRADITIONAL LAWS
Fredericton, Mi'kmaq-Maliseet Institute, 1990
    Account of the alliance of Mi'kmaq, Maliseet, Passamaquoddy, Penobscot, and Abenaki to make peace with the Iroquois, written down from oral tradition more than 100 years ago; additional articles on wampum

Nova Scotia Dept. of Education
MI'KMAQ PAST AND PRESENT: A RESOURCE GUIDE
Halifax, Nova Scotia Dept. of Education, 1997
    Detailed curriculum guide for Mi'kmaq Studies

Lisa Patterson, editor
THE MI'KMAQ TREATY HANDBOOK
Sydney, N.S., Native Communications Society of Nova Scotia, 1987
   Texts and detailed, non-technical accounts of treaties signed by the Mi'kmaq

Daniel N. Paul
WE WERE NOT THE SAVAGES: A MI'KMAQ PERSPECTIVE ON THE COLLISION OF EUROPEAN AND ABORIGINAL CIVILIZATIONS
Halifax, Nimbus, 1993
   Mi'kmaq history from the Mi'kmaq point of view; includes bibliography

Harald E. L. Prins
THE MI'KMAQ, RESISTANCE, ACCOMMODATION, AND CULTURAL SURVIVAL
Fort Worth, Texas, Harcourt Brace College Pub., 1996
   A study of Mi'kmaq survival through the past five centuries; includes bibliography and filmography

Silas T. Rand
LEGENDS OF THE MI'KMAQ (1894)
Johnson Reprint Corp., New York and London, 1971
   Ancient stories and stories about modern events and people

Darlene A. Ricker
L'SITKUK: THE STORY OF THE MI'KMAW PEOPLE IN BEAR RIVER
Lockeport, N.S., Roseway, 1997
   History and memories of this western Nova Scotia community

Ruth Holmes Whitehead
ELITEKEY: MI'KMAQ MATERIAL CULTURE FROM 1600 AD TO THE PRESENT (Halifax, Nova Scotia Museum, 1980), **MI'KMAQ QUILLWORK** (Halifax, Nova Scotia Museum, 1992)
   Two detailed sources on clothing, birchbark products, basketry, quillwork, and other arts and crafts; illustrated with paintings and photographs

Ruth Holmes Whitehead
STORIES FROM THE SIX WORLDS (Halifax, Nimbus, 1988), **THE OLD MAN TOLD US, EXCERPTS FROM MI'KMAQ HISTORY, 1500 — 1950**
Halifax, Nimbus, 1991
   Mi'kmaq stories and history from primary sources, both oral and written

Ruth Holmes Whitehead and Harold F. McGee
THE MI'KMAQ: HOW THEIR ANCESTORS LIVED 500 YEARS AGO
Halifax, Nimbus, 1983
   Mi'kmaq families and communities in the 1400s; illustrated throughout

RECOMMENDED VIDEOS — WITH NOTES
(NFB = National Film Board of Canada)

INCIDENT AT RESTIGOUCHE / LES EVENEMENTS DE RESTIGOUCHE
(NFB, 1984, #C0184 029 English, C0284-029 French; 46 min.)
   Issues of law and justice in the exercise of aboriginal fishing rights; records incidents in 1981 in the Mi'kmaq community of Listuguj (Restigouche)

JIPUKTEWIK SIPU: RIVER OF FIRE
(1991, available from producer F. von Rosen, RR #1, Lanark, Ontario KOG 1KO; 35 min.)
   Mi'kmaq oral tradition today, in stories and music, with Michael William Francis, of Big Cove, N.B.

KWA'NU'TE' MI'KMAQ AND MALISEET ARTISTS / KWA'NU'TE' ARTISTES MI'KMAQ ET MALLISEETS
(NFB, 1991, #C9191-064 English, C9291-064 French; 40 min.)
   Contemporary painters, sculptors, basketmakers, and other artists

MI'KMAQ
(CBC Halifax, 1981)
   Five videos; re-enactment of Mi'kmaq life before contact with Europeans; bilingual Mi'kmaq/English or Mi'kmaq/French

MI'KMAQ FAMILY: MIGMAOEI OTJIOSOG
(NFB, 1994, #C9194-086; 32 min.)
   Contemporary Mi'kmaq families, filmed at the Chapel Island, N.S., summer gathering by Mi'kmaq director Catherine Anne Martin

RENDEZVOUS CANADA, 1606 / NOUVELLES ALLIANCES
(NFB, 1998, #C0188-001 English, C0288=001 French; 29 min.)
   First encounters between Europeans and Native peoples: a young boy from France meeting Mi'kmaq at Port Royal, N.S., and a young Huron boy on his way to meeting European traders

THE VILLAGE OF THIRTY CENTURIES
(Beaver Creek Pictures, 1996; available from Madeline Augustine, Red Bank First Nation, N.B. EOC 1WO; 49 min.)
   Traces the history and culture of the Mi'kmaq of the Miramichi from ancient times to the present